EROS

EROS

Alberto Bevilacqua

Translated from the Italian by Ann McGarrell

STEERFORTH PRESS

South Royalton, Vermont

Library of Congress Cataloging-in-Publication Data
Bevilacqua, Alberto, 1934–
[Eros. English]
Eros / Alberto Bevilacqua ; translated by Ann McGarrell.
p.   cm.
Originally published: Milano : A. Mondadori, 1994.
ISBN 1-883642-35-3
I. McGarrell, Ann. II. Title.
PW4862.E816E7613   1996
853'.914--dc20   96-33225
CIP

Manufactured in the United States of America

FIRST EDITION

THIS ADVENTURE OF MINE . . .

This adventure of mine, made up of many loves that go with me through the present, through the life of the senses in length and breadth, through all my life, began to stir in me one day at dawn at the Rome airport. I used to go there often, when it was barely light, wandering among the glowing TV screens that announced departures for the strangest and most distant foreign lands.

A yearning to go away, to leave everything, was pushing me. But I didn't know where, my longing had no face, it was a child's caprice.

Sometimes I went so far as to pack my suitcases for the sick pleasure of this illusion which merged with the bitterness of leaving behind emotions that seemed to be detaching themselves from me, and which I saw as distant ships, about to disappear over the horizon that I watched from a shore become unlivable.

I was feeling disappointed, even by things that shouldn't have disappointed me; betrayed, not knowing by whom or by what, and I kept equivocating over shadows, seeing in each one a betrayal of the love that I was giving, that I had given. Around me there seemed to be only the carnal agitation of women, the impossibility of ever fully exploring their secret depths, and the foreknowledge that sooner or later even the most intensely loving ones would flee from me because of some fatal mistake.

I was moving inside a solitude that had no trace of peace, and even the new direction of the social life that I had to live, like everyone else, disgusted me, pushed me further away.

One morning early, in front of a luminous screen that blinked departure for some remote place, I understood what I could do; more exactly, what each of us could still do. One doesn't leave out of nostalgia, on the contrary; nor because something is over, when there are still reserves of life, of lifting wings. You can leave because of an active feeling, the only one you've ever felt: of peace, finally, of repose, your senses satisfied, disposed like notes of music from which a lovely harmony may come.

I needed to put my desires in order: living them, reliving them.

Everything has come back for a moment. The very wish, in fact, to put my desires into some order, restore their shine, polishing away any little infamies that might cling to them.

I take notes, I live, I write it all down, I remember.

And I can't say whether I'll really leave one day, on an early flight.

With some lovers it happens that you speak, you confront one another, you even evoke memories, with the sensation of confiding something to yourself.

It's as though the lover bore our psychological initials. We discover each other's identity, a perfect concord:

... I'm looking at her body. Her lips still have an ambiguous, satisfied smile, and now we are drawn together by the desire for a confession in words, following the one that has just taken place in acts, in silence.

Reading my thoughts, she asks me, "When?"

"I was ten. I would stretch out on the bed and make up fantastic things."

"Tell me."

"The things I imagined were so strong, so intense, that they were almost real. I felt that I was actually living everything in my fantasies: figures of women who would come to me, insinuating themselves, the actions which they brought to life, there in my shadowy and quiet little room, my first instincts of love, and the little room became a stage, a luminous erotic theatre. I was a little boy, but I was already thrust forward, daring and wild, into perfectly clear visions of gestures and situations which I couldn't have known at that age. It was as though an adult had taken possession of me, in order to remember experiences he had lived. The age I was then, suspended between early childhood and the beginnings of adolescence, was like the diaphanous wings and the bandaged eyes in pictures of Eros, son of Mars and Venus: the blindfold doesn't keep him from seeing; on the contrary, it lets him see in richer detail, because it's really the veil of libido, the very essence of pleasure."

"And then?"

"And then, inside me, Eros kept growing and changing. No

longer the child of the antique myths, but a youth as loving as his mother and as fierce as his father, avid, insatiable. This is how Diotima describes him in Plato's *Symposium*: full of energy, adventurous, a lover of poetry, unrivalled in sensual and sexual invention. Able to prolong his games of ecstasy thanks to the resistance and strength of his father's nature . . . In the *Symposium*, Eros is also the confidant, the thief of intimate secrets, the enemy of those who don't understand the light of his power . . . For me, then, his light was joy itself."

"Let's get back to the fantasies you were living out so vividly in your dark little room . . . Freud says Eros means that the narcissistic libido, sublimated to the pleasure principle and to reality, sharpens the instinct for survival of the individual and the species."

"Freud goes on to say that that's how libido becomes the energy that, yes, through sublimation, leads to the highest forms of spiritual life. . . ."

In her eyes I read what she is thinking, what she would like to ask me. I answer, "It's true: even then, already, as a little boy, nature let me understand the pleasure of *time suspended*, the incomparable moment when two bodies become one another."

She stretches out her arm, points to a photograph, stares at it.

"Yes, that's me, still ten years old, rowing a fake boat with my mother beside me. Back then they used to photograph children in front of painted backdrops."

Another faded photo smiles from the table, among the ones I keep as the dearest images of my life.

"Who is she?"

"That's Albina Savi. When I was a child she would take me adventuring along the banks of the Po, suggesting her own inexhaustible fantasies to me in the movements of her body, a body I still think of as a thing of wonder. The men who lived by the river used to say that she was one of the few who had a brain in her *Sister*

Gigi, which is one of our euphemisms for the female organ. She was the first woman to talk to me, to tell me her own ardent stories about curious things that brought Eros closer, and which she described as looking for the sea and seeing it even without having found it, like the mirages that explorers see, azure waters flowing where there are only arid wastes of sand.

"She told me, in fact, 'I'll do anything as long as it takes me someplace I've never been. And even if at the end you don't find what you dreamed of, what's important is that you lived out that adventure.'

"She had a religious education; then, she explained, when God failed to show himself to her, she created earthly idols of her own. She had a multitude of lovers: 'The only way to survive is to use up your life. Not being bad for the sake of being bad. But I don't know how to do anything halfway. And other people either love me or hate my guts.'

"She looked up. She saw herself in the blue heron that took flight, happy and free, from the rivery weeds, stretching out its wings against the electric blue sky. A cloud of hawks surrounded it at once. First they encircled it, making sure it knew that they were denying it any right to occupy their space, then they attacked it, striking it everywhere. It fell down onto the stones. With a last effort to rise, it beat its wings.

"Albina Savi stared at the heron. She said, 'That's going to happen to me, too . . . '"

"What does your memory of that woman mean?"

"She's the first one I ever respected, the one in whom I saw myself."

We were lying on pebbles in the dry riverbed. Naked, basking in the sun, splashing in the pools of cold water. I knew that all this could never happen again and that I would never forget the bliss that twined through us like the thread of the current through the rocks. Albina looked at the sky, and reached out her arm, so, and pulled me over against her body.

"And there I was, in front of Albina's sex. . . . ."

"So that woman was the first one you . . . ?"

"No. Everything about her was so open, so full of light, that her sex seemed no different to me from her hand or one of her white and perfect feet. Albina Savi also used to say, 'Sin is in the eye of the beholder. That's in the Bible and it's absolutely true . . . ' So true that it's remained a rule of life for me, as well."

The discovery of the female sex, in another way, came later. "And I'll tell you about that, too."

EROS IS A HAPPY MEETING . . .

When I come to know a new woman, one who is in harmony with me, I remember the nights when as a boy I watched the Milky Way.

"High in the heavens is a path we can see on clear nights. It is called the Milky Way, and it shines forth in palest brightness. Upon that path go all the gods, for it leads to the home of thunder-voiced Zeus, in his sacred realm." So says Ovid, at the beginning of the *Metamorphoses*.

I would keep watching, never leaving the window, waiting for the unknown universe to send me a presence, a sign. Pondering the *Metamorphoses*, I would repeat to myself: "Every image has to be imposed on another image, and through it become evident. We are in a universe where celestial bodies and stories are constantly changing into earthly forms and shapes, binding one another in a double spiral."

Some of Eros' best moments are when he takes delight in surprising us with unexpected happy encounters.

He offers his providence. He requires of us a free and profound faith.

CHRONICLE OF TWO LOVING ACCOMPLICES . . .

The two lovers exchange confidences in silence:

"Why keep on searching, if Eros has no soul. Sex never becomes erotic if it's without soul, at least a trace, even a breath, a ray of spirit: otherwise it's a poor wretched act. Eros is feeling oneself in such a state of confidence, of biochemical identity with the beloved, that it allows you to ignite the essence of sex, transmute the act into fantasy, into play. . . ."

"So this kind of communication between two lovers has to have reciprocal knowledge?"

"Not in any temporal sense. It's so hypocritical, so dim when some women say 'Let's get to know each other first.'

"Of course each person carries a genetic memory deep inside in which the lives that came before ours, the lives of which our life is made up — of fathers, millennia — have created layers of feelings and emotions within us. A man and woman are drawn together and let Eros be born when there exists between them a congruence of feelings and emotions already lived by other people throughout time, prompted by the present moment. And so the call is irresistible. It is this primordial identity, of which we may not even be aware, that I call the *erotic soul* . . . It can even happen the first time, one of the first times. Eros is a way of remembering our best selves together."

She admits, "I kept going from one man to another. There was a time when I'd go with anyone. I was looking for Eros. But I would come away disappointed, annoyed."

"And now? With me?"

She tells him to caress her shoulders, her thighs, her calves. Then her sex: lightly, and it opens, expands, as when with a fingertip, barely touching, one strokes the stem of a flower. Pure and essential elements: penumbra, worries and perplexities that dissolve and flee, her body melting into pleasure: "Keep doing that. And talk to me."

Words. Gestures. A surfeit and beyond. A wildness that slips into the room like a warm wind under the sill . . . It favors silences as it does confessions:

"You talk to me, too. I'll keep caressing you, but please, you talk. Tell me things. Your hottest fantasies. The most extreme sexual things you've done."

She tells him. Then it's her turn: "Now you tell me."

In these tales, some endearingly perverse, from the deepest and most secret intimacy, the life of the two lovers, never revealed till now, excites, provokes, even gives the narrow pain of jealousy an intensity otherwise unattainable: "I'm afraid of hurting you."

"Hurt me."

And then to descend along her belly as if there were minuscule crumbs to remove, brush over the groin, fingers floating between the pubis and the flesh, the dimples dewed with sweat, and then, just there, substitute lips for hand. This is Eros: to love a body, a part of the body because you understand it, speaking to it as to an expressive mind, listening to it, like the voices of a dialogue that reveals two minds made flesh, recognizing it. This lets you perceive it, discover the soul in the body's own most fleeting and hidden places, never gratified by vulgar lovers, those places which have been waiting to be revealed within the harmony of the body, the *three places*, and in the minutest folds, from which the most potent pleasure bursts forth.

As the act unfolds, the mind comes to inhabit the body more intensely, with all its possibilities of interpreting, intuiting, entreating. It's essential to respect sex rather than simply to make use of it. "Come."

She sets herself free. Orgasms. He listens to them.

The primordial depths of Eros are sending forth their signals, as from the starry deeps of a constellation the sounds of the abyss reach us at last, sometimes frightening us, changing enchantment and mystery into violence.

Possession. Eros is not, can never be, as so many men believe, purely penetration. This is profanation. To boast of penetration as a proof of strength, a manifestation of warrior virility, banishes us to the antipodes of Eros, in the realm of sexual stupidity, where penetration is often brutal and brief. Be, on the contrary, two in one, live on in this privileged state, now imperceptibly, now strenuously. Know the powerful sweetness of "feeling one another" with the adagio of controlled music until that music takes flight, until that sweetness is torn apart.

Let everything finish as late as possible. The lover can extend the beauty of the song. Ejaculation is a superfluous incident. Eros consists in the ardor or ecstasy of putting off, approaching, holding back, that which the Orientals call "the little death." Some men cast off the power contained in their semen in a few minutes. They are blind and deaf to Eros.

Eros is present, too, when each of the two lovers senses that neither is anticipating or falling behind the other's movements: they are in unison, as if they had always been inside one another.

The infallible precision of harmony. Full of wonder: "I feel you."

One of the most beautiful moments in the hours of love comes while watching the woman you have loved get out of bed; buttocks, thighs, her walk which contains the pleasure lived through, before she disappears secretly down the hall, toward the bath. It is a female vision of rare intensity, which gives body and reason to the rites of pause. . . .

Eat something, lovingly drink down the coolness of wine. Begin again.

And then toward dawn. One clinging to the other's shoulders, a dream in the hand that cups her belly, the sticky legs which fit together perfectly, the desire of bodily fusion which is everywhere, the lack of any strangeness in the other's body. The lover's body, the beloved's body, are ourselves.

This is one of Eros' sublime landscapes.

Limpid words are exchanged, about little things we love. That *sotto voce* . . . On toward sleep. Sleep like this, too, belongs to Eros, a sleep that transforms itself at last into the regret of separation. . . .

Seeing her get dressed. The forms of her body disappear. The lover kisses her, an instant before clothes begin to hide that back, those naked buttocks with the marks of joint possession, as if to possess her one last time.

Farewell. The sense of emptiness before they will see each other again.

Standing there, in front of the elevator, waiting for it to reach their floor, and another kiss, different, already holding nostalgia for the beautiful afternoon, the beautiful night, already filed in time's archives. Now it's another kind of abandon. The slow elevator is already an element of disharmony. The last kiss. Pulling apart, mysteriously, their lips have the perfume of a breath.

The door slides shut. The elevator recedes.

EROS AND PURITY

Since that day in Africa, at the edge of Leopoldville's Old Town, I have ceased to be an enchanted traveller.

The child prostitutes were going to be offered for sale in a quarter where buyers would shut them in cages with iron bars.

We came toward each other by chance, I and the line of children, along an alley that cut through one of many warrens. The little girl at the front of the line wore a ribbon in her hair. She stopped in front of me. For as long as the Love Merchant let her, she looked anxiously into my eyes, into my face, where chance had brought her as she walked.

Her child's eyes already had the tragic exhaustion of a mother consumed by life. At first I didn't understand why she had stopped there suddenly, or what her smile meant, or the bitter folds of her baby mouth. I understood when this beautiful child's right hand reached up to untie the bow that held back her hair.

The Love Merchant flapped around us, ugly and servile, urging me in wretched French, "Rape her . . . You can rape all of them if you want to."

The child was contemplating in me with regret her own future as a woman, the future she would never have. In a little while she would disappear into the cages and no one would ever remember that she had been a child with a chance of growing up, of being pretty. And so she untied the ribbon to give it to me, to leave me, who seemed the incarnation of her fantasies and her impossible hopes, a tiny remembrance of herself which might save her from being wholly lost.

A brief dialogue of gesture took place between us, containing a farewell to life. The ribbon passed from her hand to mine. Our fingers touched and clung, each of us holding the ribbon. The line of children was shoved forward. I wrapped the ribbon around my fingers before I turned back to wave goodbye.

And when I turned, I saw that she had turned back too, walking away, smiling gratefully because the red ribbon marked what was perhaps the only free gift of love she would ever be allowed.

In memory of that child I met for a few seconds, I keep the ribbon beside the photographs of those I have loved for years.

LETTER TO A FRIEND, IN WHICH I EXPLAIN "TOSCANINI'S NOTE" TO HER

". . . there are moments — when you're away, and no tension exists between us — when, thinking of you, I breathe in deeply all the satisfaction you share with me throughout these days of mine. Exactly as if I were breathing the air of a fresh new season. Thanks to you, a happy participation in all things comes back to me. I go out on the terrace, I take deep breaths, looking out over Rome, the cupolas and bell towers in the sunset, and the sunset looks at me.

These are my privileged moments. For every other passion —

including the yearning that took me through the world, adventuring through bodies which are like countries for the most part not worth exploring, so desolate and empty do they turn out to be — I substitute the idea that you exist.

It's as if we had both come back from long and complicated voyages. A human soul doesn't live only in the illusion of miraculous discoveries, like an explorer or an archaeologist, it goes on living most of all because it possesses an amazing and subtle ear, which we in Parma call "Toscanini's ear," the ability to hear a barely perceptible note, a background sound which at a certain moment rings out like soft laughter. . . .

Eros, too, who brought us together, who unites us, has slipped into us, between us, like the full and happy note of a different musical breath, after the heart has lain pinched and tight for years. We owe him something, a great deal.

I love the honesty with which you set yourself free from so many wrong turnings (before you, I never believed that a certain kind of woman could be so honest), and thus each has wed the other's passions. You will read many of those mistakes here. But they no longer belong to you, they belong to the world of other people, a crowded world, including children who, out of boredom, hurl themselves down a slide or jump from the top of a haystack. A bad fall, a nosebleed.

And so, as you read this, don't take offense. Fate is changed with a single note, *Toscanini's note*. Like falling asleep and waking. For whoever is lucky enough to find complicity, concord, also finds that a rhythmic succession of little sounds becomes the very rhythm of our life together. . . . You squeeze my hand, I feel the warmth of your fingers. There was a time when you couldn't have held me like this, when your fingers were cold and stiff, a claw. Don't be offended. . . . I think of a human being meeting another one for the first time on this earth, beginning to understand that meeting, gazing at the other as into a mirror, touching his face and his body, recognizing his similitude.

Life is of such dazzling ingeniousness, in its good and in its evil. At times the simplest means suffice: dampness and mold on the walls around a bed, for example, create little spectral realms wherein the splotches become elaborate swags of shadow, flights of black cherubim, damasks which rival the 'infernal baldaquins' of the Sun King's Versailles.

The ghostly draperies overhead have disappeared. To some lucky people it happens, as it did to you, that in a single body a woman who has often thrown herself away, who is worn out, disappointed, in some ways despicable, still makes room, as she disappears, for her own opposite, who thus is able to make for herself a fresh young heart. . . . The important thing is to be reborn from one's own ashes.

Don't take offense. What does storytelling mean, especially telling certain stories? Sometimes you need to speak alone with God, about some notion of his. Whoever feels overcome by the little miseries of humanity should go back and look in the mirror of greatness, to feel again that emotion, to be inspired by it and to ask counsel of it. Thus may you hope to find yourself again. . . ."

FIRST TIMES

I kept moving more deeply into the dense woods, furtively, silently. Among the stretches of poplars — while the river changed from azure to green to red — girls emerged from clumps of bushes, detaching themselves with a kind of joyous indolence from their partners: their bare feet moved with the cadence of the love that had just been made. Covering themselves lightly with a shirt, they went toward the stream where they spread their legs apart and crouched down to wash themselves.

Those bellies, to whose base the girls' hands lifted water with quick movements, and the buttocks which rested on their heels, had the shape of those musical instruments the lutemakers of Padua created in their fog-drowned shops, warm in ancient winters, where suddenly the bell at the entrance might jangle, but where for the most part there reigned such an awkward silence that one really felt at least the need to hum.

In these females, furtive like me, I perceived the rotundities of lutes, mandolins, violins, brought to life by thighs, knees, the channel of the backs that shivered at the water's touch.

Even now, I often leave a lamp on all night so that a sudden awakening doesn't plunge me into the nightmare of being blind. It's one of the night terrors I have suffered since I was a tiny child. Once, during the war, when we were refugees at Po, I woke up and couldn't see the light; the lamp was covered by the shape — which seemed gigantic to me — of a woman, one of Mussolini's Black Brigades. She was standing by the bed; in her left hand she had a pistol, with the right she was lifting the sheet off my legs.

Then, little by little, in the halo that swathed the uniformed woman's profane gesture (now with her gloved hand she stroked my belly, now delicately held my penis), I could see my mother's eyes, and then her narrowed lips, her nails squeezed so tightly they were white.

She leaped, striking the woman in the back, digging those nails into her forehead like a tigress. The lamp shone on me again, fully, with the impassive protectiveness of a holy image.

≈⊗

I keep a photograph of a woman's sex.

Ligabue carved it into the trunk of a poplar tree, one of the highest ones near the village of Baccanello Po. I'm sure it must still be there, because no one knows it's Ligabue's work. It's one of the sculptures (so he called them) that Liga scattered through the poplar groves on his *red motorcycle days*, his days of crazy rage. The painter used Ada Vitali as his model several times in paintings where lions, tigers, and leopards open huge fanged jaws that seem on the point of devouring the painting itself. I know that some of these jaws are the transfiguration of Ada Vitali's sex.

Liga came up the riverbank, he liked the boy I was then, he revved the engine and made his motorbike rear like a horse, and said to me, "Come on, get up here!"

We came to the tree, and I walked around it, following in his steps, circumspect, as he was, until we were in front of the sculpture. The genitalia were reproduced in the greatest detail. They plunged between the barely sketched thighs, reminding me of the sections of an orange split open to reveal the way they join the central pith. The labia hung beside the vulval fissure like a swallow's tail, the color of the wood's rosy pulp.

"See?" said Liga, pointing.

Time and the seasons had completed the artist's work. Summer thunderstorms and violent hail had erased the carving's virginal patina. Autumn rains had patiently carved out the wrinkles that nature ramifies in the secret places of a woman's body. Winter frosts, in addition to widening the fissure, had opened cracks, accentuating the tumescence of the labia, lifting the mons veneris and the nymphs into higher relief.

And moss had grown, scattered and darkened, intimating pubic hair. Some rodent had burrowed inside. Even the white birds that dived for frogs, and the fisher-martin and the blackbird, all had added touches of verisimilitude. Another hint — this time of fecundity — came from butterflies that had deposited fuzzy eggs as luminous as fireflies. It was as if all the inhabitants of the Po had brought some contribution.

Thoughtfully Ligabue began to stroke his sculpture, and within it, the intimate part of Ada Vitali. "Ada," he said, and he was not the only one, "has the most beautiful sex in the Po valley."

I contemplated him, with his dream, in the light touch of his fingers on the carving, as if he were gathering up the living, the most human essence, of the signs he had cut into the wood. He loved that sex as if not he but nature herself had created it, offering him in that moment the joyous gift that Ada Vitali had always denied him.

≫

Women are curious about my first time with a woman.

"It was at Ghiare," I tell them, "a little village so close to the river that you see it in the water."

It used to be a town of scythe sharpeners. They would sit in a circle with their legs stretched out, holding the handle vertically between their knees, then they would set the blade and pound it with their rounded hammers. You could hear the clanking all through the countryside.

When we would go past in the bus down the highway my mother would show me the glinting blades, as if the horizon were sending out sinister signals. She told me that that was where the *done gabjane*, the seagull women, lived, flying free but feeding on garbage. For the first time I heard the word "whore" pronounced with hatred. Those women, said my mother, ate men up, devoured them; they were the personification of death, and remember that he carries a scythe, the symbol of the town of Ghiare.

One evening I told my mother, "I'm going to Ghiare."

I was just fourteen.

I went back there many times.

My mother bowed her head and clenched her hands. It was her stubborn way of simultaneously being opposed and yielding to a situation about which she could do nothing. After having resounded all day long, the village seemed to remake itself in profound silence. Scythes everywhere, in long rows against the walls; in crossed bunches, like rifles, in the midst of fields, leaning from balconies, looking like the beaks of cormorants; immersed in tubs of water and abandoned in cold ovens where they had been passed through fire. The moonlight made them glitter.

I wandered through the little streets, imagining that I was in the kingdom of Death who, having laid down the tools of his trade, put off for a moment his flight across the earth. Through closed shutters, I could hear the scythe-sharpeners snoring, children crying, the pendulum of a big clock in someone's kitchen.

I tried to imagine the *gabjane*. They said they came in all sizes and ages, some were even little girls.

One night, a woman's cry drifted down from one of the last windows in the village. An orgasm. I waited. In the grey light a man came out. He pulled on his raincoat and saw me. He read in my young boy's eyes that I would have liked to go up there too, but that I wasn't brave enough.

And so he came toward me, pulling his hands out of his pockets, stretching them toward me. His big palms came close to my face, and I understood what he was doing. Half in complicity, half sarcastic, he wanted me to smell them. There was no vulgarity in his gesture; it was, rather, an offer of initiation. Then he jumped onto his bicycle and went away, pedaling energetically under the poplars.

I made up my mind and went into the house. A corridor led me on between closed doors. From the only one ajar, the voice of a woman who had heard my hesitant steps called me to her. She had pinned a silk robe across the bedside lamp which bathed her in shadowy light, altering her face.

"Come," she said, when I was close enough to recognize her, with a sense of wonder that overcame my fright. She lifted the blanket, uncovering the side of the bed next to her body.

It was Ada Vitali.

I spent that night in Ghiare, and the next day I kept trembling. I closed myself in the bathroom and kept looking at my penis.

My mother began to wait up for me.

"Come," she said it too, now with a sweetness I had never known in her. She took me into the bathroom. She unbuttoned my pants and looked closely. She washed me carefully with soap and water, and then sprinkled on something from a bottle. It burned. I let her do it.

Later I understood that this was no mere fixation, but the greatest act of maternal love she had ever shown me.

FEBRUARY. MILANO. 1982

Hotel Marino Scala.

She screamed so loudly that I jerked my head back away from her face, as if her cry could break my eardrum. Her orgasm washed over me, giving me the little thrill of triumph I used to feel as an adolescent, in certain lucky moments. The marvel of human bodies is that each one comes most fully to life through another. And no one can say I haven't loved my own.

I remember that woman's orgasm as the fullest and most powerful one I ever provoked.

And afterwards, sitting in an armchair across the room, I began to scrutinize the naked body of the young photographer sleeping crossways on the bed. We had hardly spoken during these days we had passed closed up in the hotel room where we made love, pausing only to eat something, for a short nap. We had communicated with stubborn, hot, sometimes ferocious intensity, uniquely through her orgasms.

And these orgasms through which she bound me to her — always striving beyond, always going more deeply, into the synthesis of two bodies — stirred something in my memory. I remembered a butterfly that had come into my studio one night, drifting from a plant on the terrace, drawn by the lamplight. That single bright stain suspended in the darkness must have appeared as a goal enclosing all the attraction of a lifetime, into which it had to plunge. I watched it flutter around the light and I divined the amazement and terror that must be possessing it. Then it clung swiftly against the glass, opening its wings in all their fullness, and, obedient to fate, tried to pass through the light.

While I watched, the incandescent surface sucked out the beauty of the dying colors, which did indeed give the illusion that it was passing through the glass barrier of the bulb. I remained fascinated by the secret strength that beyond all logic forces us to dive deeply into a physically alien reality.

I stared at the young photographer in her exhausted sleep, arms and legs flung out, as if mortally wounded.

A milky light filtered through the shutters. It was a cold winter, the streets were frozen, ice everywhere outside. Milano reminded me of certain bitter winters in my village. Eels and luminous aquatic grasses were enclosed in wrappings of ice that we had to break open with an icepick. Seagulls dove on the dead morsels with wings that steamed in the frosty air and beaks that opened and closed with the effort of flying while managing the weight of the cold which brought them low. We would light huge bonfires along the riverbanks, and clouds of sparrows would swoop so closely they almost touched the flames before they went back up to the sky comforted by the heat.

The body of the weary young photographer moved slightly, making tiny adjustments; a barely perceptible lament passed her lips. Her vagina, dilated and reddened, was a wound among the bruises of her inner thighs, as though a sadist had knifed her there.

Then I remembered, too, the *death of the puttana.*

At Po, this was still during the war, they brought a wounded woman to our house. I didn't know who she was, and I never even asked my mother. For me she was once and forever the singular vision of a wound: blood red, black-bordered, from her breast to her navel. Looking entirely similar to her sex which no one was bothering to cover. As if her body had two vaginas.

My mother was tender with this unknown woman, who couldn't respond because she never regained consciousness. She would stay closed in the room with her all day. At night, she told me to come in. I saw her kneeling and I knelt too. The woman was in bed, with pillows supporting her back. The light from the bedside lamp fell on the visible wound and on the other one I had half-seen. The body smelled of musk and alcohol. Her hair was drawn back, her temples hollow, her nostrils broad; she had a jaw like stone.

The head of an obscene queen, already carved for her sepulcher.

I understood that my mother's attitude of adoration was directed at the wound on her breast, but also to its resemblance to the other. Her mind, where the first sick thoughts had begun to wander, read in the two wounds a contorted analogy between obscenity and death.

Her index finger traced the great wound with a sensual hesitation, then her index and her thumb rubbed some liquid mixed with blood.

"She's dreaming," she murmured.

"What's she dreaming about?" I asked. It seemed to me that the dream must be shining out of the dense drops of sweat on that forehead, like nothing I had ever seen before.

"The Dissembler."

I didn't know what that was.

"The master of murderers and whores. But he knows how to change himself into Orlando Innamorato."

For the first time in my life I listened to her tell me about Orlando Innamorato, and what exactly a whore is, one who has the courage to be what she is, without hypocrisy, true in her own desperation, in her doubleness which lets her pass from repeated bestial couplings to the purest love. I heard the word *troia*, a sow, a trollop, my mother's voice, so calm and good, explaining it all, and I began to see that the illness in her brain was like a voracious spider, and that she, like me, alternated excessive modesty and puritanical shyness with speech that was saved only by her extreme sweetness of tone from being shameless, shocking.

There came a night when the drops of sweat disappeared from the brow of the unknown wounded woman. And I asked, "Is she still dreaming?"

"About everything there is. But she can't see it anymore."

At Berceto in the province of Parma, they have unveiled a monument unique in the world: TO THE VICTIMS OF GOSSIP AND ENVY. A brass plaque, two antique stone columns.

I went to the inauguration wearing my party dress, as we say here ironically; I even wore a hat. Only in my town, only in this land of mine, bizarre and improbable happenings which nonetheless have their own mad logic, only here could anyone think up such a monument. The people here know the wonders of the possible, the language of the eccentric and fantastic which frees us from the many enslavements we endure in other realms of life.

A crowd had begun to gather around me. The victims of the culture of suspicion all seemed to be wearing their party dresses, too; they were certainly all wearing hats.

We glanced at each other. And those glances were words, questions:

"Excuse me, why are *you* here?"

"What about you?"

The official voice rang out: "To the victims of slander, the city erects. . . ."

My own intimately private life had been the victim of wicked speculation, of every kind of unfounded fantastication, of indecent gossip which was nothing but the expression of the filthy brains that formulated it.

I remember one day with Roberto Rossellini, who could have been here with us today in his own party dress. We were alone, sitting across from one another, for very bitterness unable to put a line on paper. And Rossellini said to me, "This vile Italy, capable of turning you into pig meat, doing that to a human being only because they know his name. They invent around you every shameful thing they carry inside themselves, inside their souls."

Pig meat. The Italy of pig meat. . . .

Among persons who have never known me at all, I am described as an incontinent heterosexual, a homosexual, and anything else that comes to mind. Women I have declined, who have never been with me, and others with whom I have exchanged not one word and who have never even seen me, have invented and spread the vilest stories. My ideal of Eros, which I have sought to interpret as a poet, has been confused by the ignorant with its contrary: a squalid sexual avidity. And all this has come from men and women who will commit any baseness in order to sink a penis into a vagina, or to be penetrated.

I was shaken out of these reflections when a choral shout rose up from the crowd. An *I* in the name of everyone: "I curse you!"

≫

My way of cursing degenerate slandermongers consists in a secret rite of my own. When I came back to Parma after many years, I returned to the abandoned chapel I had bought and kept for myself, where at one time I had taken refuge when the nausea from a sea of females and males seeking nothing but insane couplings was at its peak.

I stood at the foot of a stairway that has not the slightest solemnity. Worn steps lead up to an unadorned room with damp-stained walls, a bit of air coming through a tiny window. This was where I came when I wanted to speak secretly with the purity I knew I had, that I know I have; away from the eyes of the world. This dialogue was like the special love between a betrothed couple.

There isn't any electric light, and so I lit the candle and set it on a little wooden table. It seemed to me, as always, that the ironic and melancholy Figure of my own purity was crouching nearby, waiting for me to turn on the single modest machine that I had brought into the timeless chapel, an old gramophone. I cranked it into action.

≈

I listened to the luminous "Crucifixus" from the "Credo" of Mozart's *Coronation Mass*. And when the soprano began the "Agnus Dei," which in the shadows of an ancient country church would make anyone dream, I dipped the pen that I'd used to write my first poems, and wrote out the message that I would have liked to broadcast:

"I welcome the evil things you say about me with joy, because the purity I believe in is such that it flows, limpid and unchanging, even from the wretched and deathly husks of your bodies. Death takes on everyone's identity, yours, too . . . I leave you to the vaginas you dispense to anyone at all, to several males a day; to the members whose return to erection you so anxiously entreat, every time. Don't look for reasons, you are miserable creatures who have never known the joys of love . . . And yet I'm sorry for you because you know nothing. The sacrilegious have no idea that a remarkable providence has led them to serve God's own design, causing us to look in the very face of that which we find repugnant. . . .

"He was and still remains the matrix of the starry vault that consoles us in the depths of night. What can you know about it? You're worse than animals.

"But I give you my thanks, because you have allowed me, despite all you have tried to do to me, to accomplish the miracle which is always that of being alive, of bearing the frightful and distinguished weight of life itself. . . ."

No one would ever see these inkstained pages. Only the moon illuminated me, across from the candle that was all but burned out. Mozart's *Ave Verum Corpus* was being diffused through the chapel. I turned toward the window, toward the night, and said foolishly, "Do you hear it? The purity of faith? . . . And that note, listen, listen: like the others, a tiny mark on a score, but it's ineffable because of the simple fact of its being played, of the divine gift of being set among all the other notes, as harmony requires before it can become sublime. . . ."

THE EROS OF VIOLENCE AND REVENGE

A few days earlier Claudia had told me how her adolescent dreams had been smashed forever.

At thirteen, she was shaken by the beating of her own heart when she gazed out at a certain point on the shimmering horizon of the sea. In the hazy blue of the distant water, it seemed to her that there emerged and took shape the vision of her future life. It became the outline of a sailboat, listing sideways, rocking on the waves, sometimes darting forward. She knew it was waiting to send her a mysterious message.

She used to walk toward the Sailboat, her own dream, even while she was beginning to understand that in the illusions, the imagined things of the world, she could hear something like the sirens' song. She let herself be drawn toward them. She would wander through fields, get lost down hidden roads, along the riverbank and the gravel pits. Telling herself that a certain orchard was France, that the Levante canal was Holland. And on and on, hurrying ahead, enchanted by a kind of light or a magical green or a song that sounded foreign and perhaps was, because so many of us departed for strange lands and then came back, like Marco Polo. Claudia told herself that the Venetian part of the Po was China, or who knows, mysterious Persia; the Canalbianco basin was the North Pole; the Abbey of Pomposa was all the Orient.

In the Abbey you can see, painted, the apocalypse of humanity.

But hers, at thirteen years of age, did not take place there. What would the Apocalypse be for a girl with a quick clean mind in a body already dressed in the magnificence of flesh with which Nature had favored her?

She was a squirrel caught in a snare. The heart's hair waited at the heart of luxuriant woodlands. A man was blocking her path: Armando, known as the Circassian for his heavy features and his eyes with a predator's cruelty.

This must be the Land Beyond, the travelers' tales always say it's destiny, thought Claudia. But she could not pass because the man, guessing she was hungry, told her not to be afraid, told her to come into his restaurant nearby:

"You can have a grownup meal, have some wine like a grownup, too."

He played waiter, served her lunch. When she was sated and a little bit drunk, he enticed her upstairs to a room from whose window she could see how wonderful the Sailboat was, the one that might or might not be real, the one she had told him she was seeking.

And there he violated her.

Threatening her, afterwards: "Look out. Don't ever say a word about what happened today, not to anybody. Because your brother's a delinquent, and you know it. And you know what your

mother is, too. And I can have them shot anytime I want to."
Armando the Circassian, chief of the local thugs, looming over her
as she huddled in terror on the stained bed.

≈

. . . Twenty years from that day. Claudia told me, "I've ordered a gigantic meal today at the Circassian's restaurant. Come with me.
You'll sit at a table nearby and pretend to be an ordinary lunchtime
client. You won't even know me."

"Why?"

"Because I want you as a witness."

The restaurant had a blue and white striped awning at the entrance. It seemed alert, watchful. Inside, nothing had changed. It
was the stagnant dead hour of afternoon, and if men kept coming
in and out, it was only to stare at Claudia. On the day she had endured his rape, she had seen them laugh knowingly with the
Circassian and then go out, whistling through their teeth, leaving
him free to act.

The cook had executed her orders. The lunch was as Claudia had
described it, and from serving carts all around her table there arose
a stupefying fragrance of food. Armando greeted her, said he was
pleased she had remembered his place after so long, smiled,
winked:

"You look great. Beautiful as when you were a kid, more beautiful, even. . . ." He added with subtle perfidiousness, "You haven't
been around in all these years. I thought you were dead."

"I was, but it was a long time ago."

≈

Claudia glanced up at the stairway that led to the rooms upstairs:
the same gray steps, the same landing with the diffused grayness

of the dirty glass doors. She kept to herself the thought that had obsessed her for so long: "I'll come back, Circassian, and everything will happen exactly as it did that day, but in reverse, because you're going to take my place." She began looking at the man again, finding him burdened with years and infirmity. His predator's eye now had an obscene glint that didn't come from his perverted mind but was projected there. She understood where it came from: from the little mirror Death was using to tease and dazzle him.

The man looked boldly at her legs. "How do you keep looking so good? My legs are starting to go, my heart. . . ." Insinuatingly, after a pause, "How many lovers have you got, eh?"

"And you? Do you still go after little girls?"

I saw him jerk back for a moment. Then the predator's look lit up once more. "I can still manage. Don't think I can't."

The man didn't quite understand that Claudia was magnificent in revenge, too. And that the vengeance destined for him had been planned by her from the moment it had been deserved, while she touched with a trembling hand the mess of sperm and blood that was flowing down her leg. And now she sat at the table and ordered, "Serve me!"

He obeyed. He moved heavily now, having already had two heart attacks, but they still called him Armando the Circassian and bore respect to the obscene male he used to be. He could not draw back from the challenge that now seemed predictable to him.

"Serve me," repeated Claudia. "And serve yourself. You're my guest, you have to do honor to me and to our lunch together."

Eating and drinking, she goaded him to eat and drink with the same avidity she feigned. From time to time he said, "You know, I really shouldn't. . . . ." Each time he said it, she filled his glass.

And he went along with it. This is what he wanted: to show her that he was still superior to her, to make her understand that these excesses didn't frighten him, even if he was risking his life while Claudia risked nothing.

She smiled: "Come on, stretch yourself, are you afraid you'll strain something? What do you care? Just this once. . . ."

He remembered the tearing pain that twice had lacerated his heart, but he didn't stop gulping down the tidbits of pork she held out to him, laughingly, on the end of her fork, and he too forced himself to laugh before opening his mouth, thinking to himself, Just this once, sure, and he could be Armando the Circassian more than ever. The news would spread to the four winds and he could live off this story to the end of his days.

≳

Claudia urged him on: "Come on, eat, you need to warm up your blood. If you don't . . . how will you manage when we go upstairs?"

They both looked at the stairs. He told himself that he must not let her take the initiative. "Remember?" he said with his twist of a smile. "Remember how it was, Claudia?"

"The key!" she ordered, holding out her hand.

He lifted the key out of his pocket. Holding it with two fingers, he dangled the piece of wood with "ten" written on it in red, the number of the room. "Number ten. Remember?" He was pleased with his performance so far. He was standing up to her. He had even worked into his voice the same deceitful tone that had worked that earlier day, when he had the child Claudia, her cheeks flushed with food and wine. He had swung the wooden tag back and forth, holding the key while he told her: "Come on. From my room that Sailboat you think you see is so close you can reach out and touch it. . . ." His voice was almost the same now: "So you still believe in crazy sailboats?"

"I came back here because I believe in them more than ever. If we're both here, it's because neither of us has ever changed what we believe." She got up, started up the stairs, commanding him, "You can bring the bottles."

The Circassian loaded his arms with bottles. Dragging himself up the stairs behind her high heels, his veins felt full of lead, he felt nauseous. For very few women had he ever felt the boundless hate that this one provoked in him by being so boldly a woman, so sure of humiliating him with her mocking magnificence, swinging her hips just in front of his eyes. Challenging him, whose lust had been driven by a dream that sometimes came when he was wide awake: to walk through the poplar groves some morning and see a woman hanging from every tree.

Claudia left the door open. Just enough for someone to see inside.

They faced each other in the room with its bed. Ten years younger, thought the Circassian, and I wouldn't have a dry mouth and my tongue heavy as a marble stone. Just the same he grabbed the glass she offered him, who's counting, drank it down in a single gulp, and took the next one too. His tongue loosened and he could speak again.

"Your health," she said.

" . . . Health," he managed to say.

She pushed him and he sat heavily on the bed. He had expected it. Claudia's plan was clear: she wanted them, roles reversed, to reenact every situation of that distant day. He had pushed her, too, grabbing her while she looked out the window at the sea, laughing a little, complaining that she was dizzy (his own head was spinning now), that she couldn't focus on the Sailboat. And he had said, "Take off your clothes, don't be afraid. I just want to look at you!"

31

He started clawing at his clothes, pulling off his shirt and sweater with some difficulty, while he heard the same words: "Take off your clothes. I just want to look at you." He swore then, "Dammit!" Because, overwhelmed with nausea again, he had to bend over: the exact reaction that the child Claudia had had. She could see the scene again, exactly as before: she where he was now, her back naked and stiff, her face covered with red splotches; as she turned her eyes she saw that he quickly covered up his own, reflected in the mirror across from the bed. Then he realized that the woman, with perfidious gentleness, was lifting up his feet, stretching him out, making sure he was framed in the mirror.

He had always liked forcing a woman into that funereal position before he made use of her: "Relax, let me help you," he had told the little girl Claudia.

And now the woman, sarcastically, "I'll help you, just relax."

Armando wasn't quick enough to stop her. Stupefied, he noticed that she had taken hold of his belt, that she was stripping off his clothes with the same swift and imperious gestures that had made him invincible as a young man. But lying down like that he felt better.

"I'm old," he said to her, full of poison. "I'm disgusting, I know. What satisfaction can it give you? It's only fair and natural that a sick old man. . . ."

Looking impassively at the ruined body, Claudia interrupted him. "I didn't come here for satisfaction. But I do want everything to fit in a logical way. You, today, are too old. I, then, was too young. What difference does it make to the one who's getting the profit?"

He tried to resist her, but his eyes felt like stones and he couldn't keep staring into the void; he glanced at his penis and scrotum where she too was staring without expression.

"Look at it. It's dead," she told him. "Don't you see it's dead?"

It was indeed a little puddle of dead meat, no matter how vigorous and prompt it had once been, so much so that his obscene and carousing friends used to call it *the idol* or *the beast*, the Circassian's beast. A dark liquid oozed from under his eyelids, perhaps tears of defeat, or perhaps simply a sign of his illness, like the sweat flooding his face. And still he spoke defiantly, "All the same, mine was the first one to get inside you, Queenie. The one that made a woman out of you!"

Claudia's voice was neutral. "Exactly. That's why this was all I wanted, Circassian. For both of us to look at it, see it dead." She filled the two glasses to the brim. "Let's drink together to seeing your dead thing." She raised her glass and gave the other one to him. He tipped it over, slopped it on himself. The Circassian laughed: "You haven't beaten me yet. There's plenty of time for it to come back to life." His right hand shot up under her dress. She quickly blocked his wrist, squeezing it between her knees, hoping to break it. He bore the pain and went on. "They say you're a woman who can bring dead men back to life again. Well, show me, do it!"

She relaxed her knees and his hand flopped down beside the bed. "That's one miracle that's impossible. How can anybody resuscitate something that's never had a life of its own, a carrion animal's piece of rotten meat?"

The man's eyelids opened, showing eyes like glowing embers. His hand took hold of his member with the bold strength of long ago, gripping the idol so many had found awesome in the old days of drunken laughter and brute revelry. An avenging idol does not die, does not forget its worshippers. And he had adored it with the most repugnant rites, eager for any baseness that would satisfy its will. How could it deny him the miracle?

She picked up the glass the man had overturned. She set it beside hers on the night table, filled them both. Sitting on the side of the bed with her back to him, she said, "Go on. Fine, I'll wait to drink the toast."

The bed was shaking. Of the man, Claudia could see only his feet, two blades of tendon and bone, thrust out from the rigid legs. From them she divined what effort the Circassian was expending on himself to try and make the idol rise up from his carcass, rebelling at the humiliation of being wrung like the neck of a rooster incapable of spreading its tail to charm a hen.

The man laughed at that image, melancholy, shaking his head. Then he tried to concentrate on the visions that had most excited him in his life. With his head thrown back, he could feel the idol approaching. . . . He didn't understand immediately that the fire in his arteries was not the idol of his moments of glory. With a feeling of triumph, he gripped something that was not an erection, but that which he suddenly recognized as the poise, the rising coil of the venomous serpent that slithers through the undergrowth of the heart before it finally strikes.

The serpent was crawling up from his stiffened feet which felt like ice. He had to block it in time; the doctors had told him to let every part of his body go limp, as if he were playing dead, so that the real death would be fooled and go away. Claudia heard, "Help me."

She turned and saw the Circassian with arms and legs flung out as though he were falling through nothingness, and from some pit he looked up at her, beyond fright, with a mad faith, making her understand that now she herself was the only idol, capable of a miracle.

"Help me not to die."

She was disconcerted for an instant, until she remembered words her mother had told her many times: real cruelty is being able to boast of having done a favor. She took his hand and held it, trying to transmit to him with her touch, her look, the same strength which she had brought here to kill him; now trying to stop the serpent before it struck his heart. . . . There were still a lot of surprises in this road company of a world, a garland of plot twists and changes. If anyone had told her as she set foot in the restaurant that her fingers and the Circassian's would be clinging to each other in desperate solidarity, and that she would be urging him. . . .

"Come on, Circassian. . . . You can do it, Circassian."

For the first time, the man felt sentiments pass through him: absurdity, love, human gratitude, if he were spared; feeling a little of everything, feeling that the game was worth the candle. Everything had been so lacking in him until now that, because of this faint illumination, the grace of survival would now not be denied him.

He looked at the light filtering through the red wine in the two glasses on the table beside him, at that splendor which seemed to enclose the essence of life as it flowed back into him without any idol, forcing the serpent backwards until it departed from him.

"Now," he said, risking the strength a smile required, "the toast."

Claudia drank the wine in her own glass. She set the other on the Circassian's chest and went out of the room.

The Circassian kept staring at himself in the mirror across the room, balancing what looked like a long-stemmed flower, a boutonnière with a crystal corolla, just over the place the serpent had not quite reached.

"You'll think this is crazy," I tell her, "but jealousy, for me, was a kind of conquest. My childhood, my adolescence, were so difficult, love touched me so rarely — even my mother's, so sick with anxieties and anguish and phobias, always someplace else, always far away in some clinic — these desolate wastelands of my youth gave me the habit of accepting the love of others no matter how it came, even if it was unhealthy or unattainable . . . Only afterwards, late, did I learn to show real feelings, authentic emotions. And at the same time I learned the fear of losing them, the will to defend them, the right to know they were absolutely mine. . . ."

"So, isn't jealousy the tendency to blame your companion for sexual infidelity without any foundation? In the 'delusion of jealousy' Freud saw a defense mechanism against strong homosexual tendencies. It's almost as if there's some tormented and sullen need for another man, another woman to come into the relationship and exist so that we can have an unconfessed desire for that person."

"Jealousy gets burdened with a lot of ponderous theories that it doesn't deserve, most of them absurd. How can you not be afraid that someone might steal away the person who makes you happy? Or more precisely, setting aside the actual person, how can you not fear your happiness being taken away?"

"All the same, jealousy is the feeling that makes one most vulnerable, most unhealthy. . . ."

"There isn't a single strong feeling that doesn't have something unhealthy about it. And then, too, jealousy is a privileged state because it switches on the world of the fantastic, the imaginary. It's richly creative. I can tell you some of the fantasies that two lovers tell each other. These tales of Eros. . . . Creativity doesn't have any limits. It can be brilliant and, for that very reason, agonizingly painful. It always exacts a high price. You get scorched when the marvelous invades your being, it makes you feel the very breath of God, but hellfire, too. Jealousy makes you feel alive, and feeling alive is always accompanied by the dread of death. In this sense, jealousy can become pathological, and its pathology can assume the most unthinkable forms."

"When were you jealous for the first time?"

"When the right to love, as I've told you, came back to me after a long time of feeling nothing. A girl asked me, 'Touch me, caress me. Just touch me.' And I touched her face, her body, everywhere, in a long, meticulous caress, and I realized that my hands were able to make her feel wonderful, so wonderful that her whole body seemed to be filled with light, illuminated, as if her smile were spreading from her lips to every part of her . . . She wasn't my woman; being with me she was betraying someone else, but even though I was the traitor, I felt such an intense regret at the idea that another man, other men, could touch her as I had done, and that she would start to glow with secret light again. . . ."

Suddenly a memory grows inside me, contradicting me. A memory I had always kept at bay:

"Or no, maybe that wasn't the first time. I was a little boy, my mother wasn't sick yet. She used to dance wonderfully, when she was young; she loved to dance. I can see that place as if I were there right now: *Ballo Gardenia*, the Gardenia Ballroom. I have the clearest vision of my mother's last dance, before her sickness. Everyone wanted to dance with her. And she was dancing now with one, now with another, and I was sitting by myself, watching her be happy having forgotten me, not noticing, in her joy, that I was there too, right there — and I'd gone to the Gardenia Ballroom with her to see her, after all, being happy. I felt like a betrayed lover, and at the same time I was proud of having a feeling that I took to be adult. When one of her friends playfully grabbed me and dragged me onto the dance floor, I moved with uncertain steps, not sure whether I wanted to weep or be proud. That child's steps, keeping time to the gay music in order to fight the pain of his exclusion while he savors the sick pleasure of revenge, still move inside of me; I feel them, always, hesitating through the Dance of Jealousy."

EROTIC FANTASIES: TALES TOLD BY EROS

Lovers exchange them while they're making love. Or else each of the two keeps them, secretly, in the mind. These fictions are part of the physiology of Eros: to tell them to one another is to partake of communion; to hide them and follow them instead of thought is something alien, mental reserve. Often they're ingenuous, childlike, like fables, after all. Yet telling these things to one another takes us back to a childhood state, to dreams of gnomes, fairies, plots we invented as children, unless someone else invented them for us.

In the fables of Eros, the childish has its own way of transforming itself into transgression, into some tiny perversion. And thus our darkest parts are exorcized, even certain longings for betrayal. The complicity created through recounting our fantasies dissolves the obscene margins which spread like pale stains around the thoughts of lovers. These almost never translate into real actions, at least not unless reciprocal viciousness takes over.

Fantasies make up one of the most dangerous and controversial chapters of Eros. With a touch of irony and benevolent connivance, I relate here a few which many women admit sharing with their lovers. One of the most common examples: "At the movies, you're beside me, and in the seat on the other side of me a man I don't know sits down. He starts reaching up under my skirt, stroking my legs. His hand goes up along my thighs, first furtively, afraid you'll notice. And you pretend not to see that hand that keeps slipping higher, pulling my panties aside, and I let him, I let him do it. . . ."

The woman who told me this would never, in reality, lend herself to this kind of degradation. Were she importuned in such a way she would react with violent outrage.

The exceptions may suffer uncontrollable consequences.

I read a newspaper headline about a murder. A thirty-year-old woman has been killed in Rome; mysterious circumstances: "LYDIA WAS ASKING FOR IT," announces the headline. The story dwells on her sick and secret relationships: a long tale of dangerous games. Her husband never knew. One of Lydia's lovers would take her to adult movie houses where she would perform sexual acts with various unknown men while her accomplice looked on, directing her performance.

Some fables of Eros help us surmount the terror of such aberrations. It isn't true that a healthy woman doesn't suffer anxieties like this to some degree. In fact, she *is* healthy and honest because she recognizes her own yearning for fear and pain without yielding to contamination. What limpid recognition is unaccompanied by the fear that negative forces might reach inside her and destroy her? Even a woman's fidelity may endure fantasies of contradiction and temptation:

"I want to make love to you someplace where anybody could walk in on us, see us. I want someone to see me now, right this minute."

A "masculine" proverb says that the form of a woman's vagina can be intuited by the shape of her mouth. But according to a "feminine" proverb, a man's endowments can be read in his hand, the shape of his fingers. Two rules that are never wrong, or so it is joyously affirmed. And now watch the play of glances between two lovers during a dinner party, their looks which intersect, straying to the hands, the mouths, of the other guests.

Just as in childhood games, the fables of Eros don't always need words.

The obsessive "other woman," "other man" recurs.

"How do you think I'd be with another man?"

"Do I get to have another woman?"

She's upset. Sometimes she gets angry.

In the film *Empire of the Senses*, the most disturbing scene is the one in which the protagonist, beginning to crack because of his lover's endless challenges, notices a flash of interest in the eyes of the old servant who has been attending the couple, meekly off to one side. He takes her in rage and pity, and the serving-woman dies in that final orgasm.

He asks, "Have you ever done it with a woman?"

"It happens. To a lot of women. And you, with a man?"

Men are generally horrified by this question. But there are those who admit their own occasional bisexuality which may have been revealed in some simple gesture, innocently, once upon a time, perhaps as a boy.

"I guess it could have happened."

Women's fantasies are often nourished by a reality that demands to be confessed, for the pleasure of the very strangeness of the experience.

"One day I was sunbathing on the beach in Africa. I was all alone except for one of the locals, an old man, waiting, all wrapped up, a hood over his head. I could see his eyes glinting in the shadow. He was crouched down like a beggar, filthy, ragged. He kept staring at my crotch . . . so, I slid my hand into my bikini, I stretched it so my whole pubis showed, I did it very slowly, right in front of him. I started to get wet. I don't think it was my own obscene gesture that excited me, but the idea that this old relic was feeling happiness he would never have dreamed of, feeling his blood course as though he were young again, desiring this strange blonde woman he dared not touch, wanting her a thousand times more than the money he was waiting for so patiently, knowing that someone would throw him a coin sooner or later, asking for nothing, unmoving under the baking sun on the beach, like a spar from a wrecked boat. . . ."

And then the woman whose fantasy is for her lover to call her by degrading names . . . and the childish awkwardness of the lover who tries to say these things to her.

And when the woman conveys the notion that she's lost in delirium, all inhibitions gone, sunk in a kind of hypnosis out of which uncontrollable truths surge forth, the man may suffer retroactive jealousy to a great degree. This surely is jealousy's most tormenting form: in this case, indeed, a self-punishing excitement is born from all that one wants — and at the same time doesn't want — to know about a woman's past, her sexual experiences. Which men. How. When. Out of that past, which may become an obsession, a thousand painful hypotheses come forth, crowded with ghosts, excesses, possible and improbable situations.

And so the fables of Eros include both their own Tom Thumb and their own Ogre. The list of complexes, defined as it happens, in terms of tale and fable, includes a "Tom Thumb complex." And the textbooks say, "The Ogre corresponds to the introjection, the psychic assumption, of the aggressor's characteristics."

The important thing is to exorcize in freedom these many and useless terrors.

Everyone in Parma had heard about this. They used to talk about it.

There was once a young woman of twenty with a very beautiful voice: Oberta Bonifacio. Her father, idolatrous because of the famous name he bore: Oberto, Count of San Bonifacio, had sired her instead of the son he had expected. Hence the name Oberta: "The thought of an unhappy love," he would explain, quoting from the slender libretto of Verdi's first opera, two acts written by Temistocle Solera. "*I was betrayed! Despairing! The mockery is not for you alone!*"

Music lovers would come from far away to wait outside the Bonifacio house. Back and forth, pretending that they were out for a stroll, the fluttering little crowd would wait patiently, glancing up at the balcony, at the drawn curtains behind the rows of geraniums.

Sooner or later Oberta would sing.

She peeped down at them. She was pleased that the feigned passersby grew into an ever more numerous crowd, but she struggled with the panic that people caused her:

"The world makes me afraid," she said.

"The world makes her afraid," confirmed her father, desolated. He attempted a justification: "The world of men is ferocious. Did it not happen that even my own ancestor, Oberto, Count of San Bonifacio, was defeated by Ezzelino da Romano?"

"Indeed, it happened," agreed the forlorn listeners.

But sometimes the long wait beneath the windows was not in vain.

Sometimes Oberta was moved by a sign that had nothing to do with humanity: it might be the light, sliding down the walls, announcing a brilliant springtime; or the perfume of lime trees which drifted in from the streets, making her dizzy; or the comic felicity of a tomcat she saw writhing on the rooftops across the way.

And then she would rush, her blood pounding, to take refuge in the recesses of the great house. To make love all alone, in the shadows of her little room, sprawled on her white bed. And when she came, when the orgasm she bestowed upon herself had armed her against her fear of the world, her great voice was set free, sending the soul of Violetta floating out over the town:

"*Tutto e' follia nel mondo — Cio' che non e' piacer. — Godiam, fugace e rapido — E' il gaudio dell'amore, —*

E' un fior che nasce e muore, — Né piu' si puo' goder!

Everything in the world that's not pleasure is folly.

Let's yield, melting quickly, to the madness of love. The flower that blooms and dies knows fleeting joy. . . ."

"Better than Malibran," they said there, down below.

"Much better," we echoed.

EROS WHEN YOU LEAST EXPECT IT

I went out into Parma in the early afternoon, in the dead hour when the streets of the provincial city are sunny and deserted.

I realized, stupefied, that I was following a woman through neighborhoods and alleys. She had a *Parmigiano* body, I don't know any other way of describing the allusiveness that animated her, thighs and shoulders inherited from a peasant father, long legs that went on so elegantly: something left to her, naturally, by her country parents who taught her to copy the movements and gestures of the landowners who had dominated their lives.

In her I was seeing generations of women who had given their milk to whole upper-class families, sexually weaning their own first-born.

43

And if I went out on my bicycle at the edge of town, once more I saw that I was beside another girl on a bicycle, pedalling with joyous energy on her way to work. The wind lifted her dress along the backs of her thighs, and I stared at that white and rosy flesh, trembling with the vibrations of the pedals' every movement.

She realized that she was being followed. And so she lifted herself imperceptibly, letting her dress rise up a little more, until I could see the ineffable line where her underpants pressed lightly across her buttocks.

She calibrated this invitation so that an ardent and reciprocal dialogue of excitement burst forth. We had to maintain a certain distance, otherwise the silent conversation would be interrupted. Desire made my heart beat, it surged into my blood and filled my senses like the perfume of the lindens along the road. And then the unknown girl disappeared down a side street.

Those Emilian girls grow up sexually trained by what I have defined on other occasions as civilization, to which Eros disguised as a bicycle seat lends complicity from the time they are very young; an involvement that takes place in full sunlight in the open air, more subtle than any masturbation without any sense of guilt, a bold and innocent transgression because it is immersed in the very necessity of being alive.

A girl confided to me, "I like to wear big skirts that the wind can get under, and the tiniest panties. I see people looking at me so happily, and I love it. And I'm excited because I'm provoking them but at the same time, I feel clean."

Don Marco, the priest from Sabbioneta, my second home, was a man about whom women always said, "women like him." But he wore a habit and this made him different in my eyes. He liked me, and he called the intelligence I showed as a little boy "a thought-less wine," like Malvasia, which nonetheless gets into your blood, darting and fizzing through your thoughts. I served Mass for him, I helped him in little tasks; for the most part I used to spend hours sitting under the willow tree near the rectory.

Giulia appeared, standing at the edge of the field.

She gave Don Marco no peace. Next she would arrange herself next to him on a bench in the church, and, adhering her thigh to his, as if to make room for a nonexistent neighbor, stretch her knees apart, fanning them by flapping her skirt, showing off her bare legs. After the swarm of pious bigots who came to morning Mass, in Giulia's presence the nave filled up with human breath, and her figure gave meaning to the menacing finger God pointed from the wall, urging mankind to turn away from temptation. Even the saints' eyes seemed brighter behind the cobwebs, and the violet sky behind their shoulders prefigured a more credible tempest.

Don Marco pretended not to notice. He bent down more fervently in prayer, or so it seemed to me, watching them both.

Then Giulia took hold of the priest's hand, pulling him through the church as if she were bearing him off to a lovers' meeting. The confessional was open and Don Marco slipped in, drawing the curtain, finding himself with the woman's beautiful face, her light breath behind the grating. Giulia pretended to be confessing, her voice full of devotion, implacable as she described in minute detail the sins of the flesh she had committed with this one or that one. Local gossip said of her, "She'll do it with anybody. Even with her father, with farm animals."

And yet her profile was purity itself, it seemed impossible that it could ever distort itself in the performance of forbidden acts, or be hidden by some beast's bewildered head.

There at the back of the church, I spied on that confession which united Don Marco and Giulia, furtive as any coupling. Imagining what she could be saying to him, I fell into a delirium of visions which grew into unbearable tension, until the violence with which my senses were responding reached its limit.

One day, the three of us were at the entrance to the bell tower. It was obvious that Giulia was wearing nothing under a loose, bright tunic, belted at the waist. She went up the stairs ahead of us. Don Marco followed her. I looked up: at her slender ankles, at the white skin of her thighs inside the darkness of her dress. I felt, as surely Don Marco did too, a yearning to reach out my hand, slip between her thighs, barely touching them, until I reached the heat that emanated from her sex, to warm my fingers at that heat, and with a gesture of sacrilegious adoration let them be lost in that pubis that seemed to us immense.

∗

I was in my car, caught in an infinity of stalled traffic in a bottleneck along the Tiber, moving more slowly than anyone could walk, at rush hour. Another car was next to me. The young woman's face appeared next to mine and we stared at each other through the closed windows.

Suddenly, and I understood this, she would have liked to look away. But she didn't. She focused on my stare, resolving some inner conflict in a fraction of a second.

I know that kind of look so well. That kind of desire.

It became a force which the girl could not control, hypnotizing her as it was hypnotizing me. Her eyelids seemed blocked over her green eyes.

I read there, in succession, contrasting emotions: astonishment, happiness at seeing me, bitterness, hope. More than anything, an invitation for us to know one another. The woman was notably beautiful. Her long gaze resisted the din of horns that began to honk, assailing us from everywhere.

Then the car moved off. Bearing away with it the unexpected recognition of Eros in that lingering look.

A musical complicity may be born between two men, a complicity that finds its orchestra in the senses, creating an ineffable bond, difficult to define. Other things creep into it: melancholy, the regret for impossible loves, for women who remain indifferent, as if they were rendered distant and extraneous by their being attracted to men in some dull or perverse way, subjugated by the world of femininity, which often turns out to be exclusive, neurasthenic, and full of itself.

It takes luck to deal delicately with women.

Between two male friends the worry about being harsh, about betrayals, simply dissolves; and an emotional relationship of deep affection may be born. It is like living molded into life, exactly like when, in a letter, you add a sentence, "just a line," wherein the heart speaks with total and reciprocal understanding, and sensuality itself, being mirrored, assumes uncommon outlines, special strength, because it is being nourished by the same, hard-won exclusion from vulgar reality.

Women do not understand which of Eros' languages will best allow two men to communicate in purity. They insist on being overly clever, and this causes them to see a lurking homosexuality. And this suspicion is a ridiculous vice that is born, in the world of women, out of a sense of caste which does not accept being displaced even as an hypothesis.

In many cases where the soul's preference is at stake, homosexuality, heterosexuality, are only convenient dogmas, fruit of a millenary manipulation of minds, similar to the various measures which at times have caused the Catholic church to exclude women from the practices of the life of sensibility and the life of the spirit.

Eros does not live by dogma, any more than human existence does. His light breaks down ephemeral contrasts, his are not the taboos and terrors that poison superficial society, that clog the quotidian. If Eros is not a god but a priest in the service of the free play of the senses, you can belong to a friend, to him and to yourself, one making space in himself for the other, with the sentiment of an unknown beloved's transmission by an intelligence that is always irregular, open to everything, that accepts the risks, that doesn't let itself be destroyed by corruption, that knows how to steep itself in sorrow while knowing how to emerge again.

A single, misunderstood soul is worth a lot. It is a magic lantern.

≫

. . . I remember how silent it was at M.'s house. We felt ourselves scrutinized by that silence, almost a look boring into us, embracing the room. We raised our heads and we ourselves looked very hard, making our eyes answer that stare which was subjugating us, to show it that we were aware of its presence and its strength.

I wanted to get up and go away. M. wanted to shut himself in a dark room and cry. At which point solitude preceded us: it changed into a siren and carried with it, across the Roman rooftops, an Oriental enchantment, which enclosed the melody of life itself when we heard it drift away from our will toward happiness.

M. turned on the stereo, music spread through the room.

Then he came toward me, caressed me. We could read in one another's eyes the infallible precision of how perfectly in tune we were; this syntony causing each of us to recognize what an immense leap in confidence he had made.

That's all. Nothing else.

Going back to Po, I rented a motorboat and had someone take me along the banks of the Puttina. The river was filled with the clearest, palest light, in which villas and gardens slid past; solitude came growing up out of the floodlands until, at my signal, the boatman stopped at a great sandbar. Beyond it there were some ruined lake dwellings on their rotting stilts.

That tract in the swampy vegetation, where the river locks were gilded with bright rust (and the sun, skimming over the reeds, made them look like the armor of Gonzaga's knights who fell by the hundreds in remote battles), used to be called *Véc Bérgniff*: the Old Libertine.

Old people came here to make love, while young couples kept their distance.

Once I saw two of them make love. They came out of the reeds of Bosco Rosso and stopped under a poplar tree. They must have decided in a hurry, thoughtlessly; so much so that he — a tailor from Cicognara whom I knew — still wore his smock, stuck full of pins. And the more he tried to embrace her, the more his companion had to draw back; there was always a new pin sticking her that had to be pulled out. The beginning, therefore, was laborious and caused the two old people much hilarity, until finally all the pins had been removed and nothing remained to complicate things.

And then they found the excuse that she had a scar on her breast. I saw them confabulate about the scar, evidently evoking and discussing its history, the timeless chattering of people their age. It must have had to do with a bitter period in her life, because the woman began to cry, even started to run away, but he took hold of her firmly, and then began to comfort her with unexpected sweetness.

They began to laugh together again, now on some silly pretext, as kids do; and it was with a casual movement that she made her companion lie down on the grass, beginning to stroke his breast, meditating the possibility of bringing their two solitudes together, not just in forced laughter but in a different complicity. At last, she too crouched down. She unbuttoned his pants, keeping herself somehow distant as she did this, almost as if she were afraid of letting her hands do something they were so unused to doing, motions from a girlhood now so distant it might be thought unworthy. She drew out his member and leaned over to scrutinize it. She had the look of someone who has learned, at the cost of her whole life, that miracles do not exist but that it's absurd not to expect a few.

The old man, too, looked at his member as it lay across his pants; looked with the same intensity crossed by a smile. First guardedly, then with cautious joy, the four hands began to touch it. This already made them happy: they were, once more, two kids who were getting ready to fly a kite; and sometimes the hands would interrupt the long caress to stroke one another, to give each other courage.

When an unexpected, vigorous erection arose, the old tailor was stupefied: they gazed at one another, at it, disoriented, not quite knowing what to do, before following the kite that went straight up into heaven, satisfying the magic trajectory of kites, anxious to see if it would list or be dragged downward by a gust of wind. They seemed to be asking themselves what mysterious force had caused it to take flight: was it their own bodies which possessed and nourished it, even though they could not know or guess, or was it instead the grace conceded by a moment forgotten in the flight of years, a little distraction in time?

The old woman stood up, going more deeply into the reeds to celebrate the act.

The old tailor followed her: he walked with the extreme attention and fluttering heart of a juggler who keeps a group of fragile objects perilously balanced in the surrounding air.

THE EROS OF RENUNCIATION

October.

It was good to be at Riano. The colors of the rooms were delicate. The villa had a park. The woods already had a few hints of autumn. The transparence of all things touched even the guests. Not far off, a little lake. I had passed almost all my time there sitting on its bank.

The first day, Flavia had followed me. I liked the way she made the silence smile. Then why was I showing how indifferent I could be?

Perhaps I had been conditioned by the speeches of the other guests. The usual: sex without soul is dominant all around us; so many men and so many women feel themselves paradoxically comforted by the fact that false sex, like theirs, is the representation of society and of life. Someone summed up the first Congress of European Sexologists: "Tired, repetitive, predictable sex. Overwhelming loss of desire. . . ."

Someone else had made ironic jokes about sexology, about theories that split hairs with a chilly scalpel, in a material that requires profound and sometimes painful involvement through personal experience, living out the reality of life: "The analysis of the carnal soul is done on your own skin, not behind a desk."

I had been thinking about the words of a French writer, among the most singular of our century and yet largely unknown, one of my favorites: Paul Léautaud.

≈

Poet of physical love, and, like Proust (whom I never wanted to read), of the difficulties of amorous communication in the contemporary epoch, he was delicious and original both on the printed page and with his eccentric lovers. He wrote: "The first country we inhabit here beneath is life, and life is contained in the desire that inspires it. Nothing is worth the sacrifice of life, nothing is more repugnant than that which snuffs out desire. One must learn to recognize this cruel spider. Cast it out. At all costs."

And now I was saying to Flavia, "Do you mind? I'd rather be alone."

She reacted mildly, with traces of respect and bitterness.

"Are you sad?"

"No," I lied.

"Is there anything I can do?"

"Nothing."

Without looking behind me, I knew that she had disappeared: hurt, humiliated. And yet I liked her so much.

I saw her again that afternoon. She was lying in the sun by the swimming pool. Unnoticed, I watched her body.

She was wearing only shorts. Much as I tried to hold back, my desire, sensually provoked, slipped through that ambiguous fissure in certitude we call wonder.

Since it couldn't be seen with me, it acted alone.

Like a cat it leaped from its peevish owner's lap onto Flavia's and began kneading her with soft paws: her breasts, her belly, the thighs where her white shorts hinted at the shadowy pubis.

Sunlight made flesh . . . Flavia stood up. I contemplated that easy walk whose very discretion stimulated me, recalling the secret rites of womanhood; I immediately associated her with other rites lost in time which I too had celebrated: the best. My desire asked, "How will she make love? Will she show off or keep herself modestly for me? In silence? Or with which words? Will she choose me carefully, or not differentiate me from casual loves?"

The other men — it was obvious — were following her with the same speculations as I.

Now it was night. The last. The guests all went upstairs. I too was in my room. The adjacent room on the right was Flavia's. She was putting things into her suitcase, getting ready to leave.

She came out into the corridor and closed her door, slamming it more loudly than necessary. Her steps paused outside my door. I heard her breathing, waiting. I reached for the doorknob. Why did I still hesitate? Was it because of that fragility, I asked myself, that can make desire disappear for no reason at all, for fear that the moment of grace, ever more difficult to accept, might vanish?

No, I admitted. It was, absolutely and uniquely, the sick pleasure of renunciation.

I heard Flavia's steps go down the stairs. The sound of her car starting back to Rome.

THE RETURN OF CONJUGAL EROS

I let her keep on following me . . .

It had been two years since I had seen my ex-wife. I hadn't even heard her voice on the telephone.

And now these steps that were echoing through a silent and deserted Rome, like the last raindrops falling on a roof, like the beating of a heart inside a body bereft of speech.

It was she, I knew it with absolute certainty. I had heard those steps behind me suddenly in the night. Like a hand grabbing my throat in the darkness. I could not mistake any others for them. Those steps, those steps alone, with their barely perceptible disharmony, remain in my very heart. They accompanied my own for many years, and my steps sought to harmonize with hers down streets through all the world; more exactly, we both sought, walking, to resolve into a common harmony two disharmonies which ever since belong to us, forever.

It's all over. The way certain conjugal relations do finish, without our really even knowing why. Only because life is as it is.

I was crossing Piazza San Bernardo and thinking about the Moses at the center of the fountain, which tradition attributes to the rash Prospero da Breccia. It is said that Prospero wanted to emulate the Moses of Michelangelo, but he sculpted the statue as it lay on the floor and when, completed, he raised it upright, he discovered with horror that he had misjudged all the proportions.

Had I, too, in the same way, carved out my whole life, my marriage? Prone, supine . . . And when it came time to render an accounting, I tried to prop them up. . . . Perhaps Marta, my ex-wife, was having these thoughts too.

At that hour there was no one else in the piazza.

I walked on, and my shoes broadcast the docile sound of my solitude. I could hear her steps echoing behind me. When I stopped, they stopped. Nonetheless, I kept pausing and going on naturally, as if she weren't there. I didn't look back, I didn't even think about looking back.

I turned into Via di Santa Balbina where — how strange, I told myself — according to the *Mirabilia Urbis* the Fire of Hope used to be lit, and the poor wretches who gazed upon it ceased their suffering. Rome is especially Christian in this way, dispensing parables like this so that the little mysteries of humankind don't end up lost in the universe of the absurd.

And here are her footsteps again. I'd thought of something: I would lead Marta home with me. Probably she, as she followed me, had been caught up in the same yearning. Having understood that I was not going to react in any way, that I would not make contact with her, Marta — I felt it — was, as I was, savoring the vague pleasure of shadowing me.

≈

Suddenly an emotion, sweet and wild, took hold of me and I remembered a night like this, lost in past time, the same date in December, ending in a gasp of winter. Tonight we were retracing the same itinerary as when we had gotten lost together the first night we went out to dinner together.

Coming out of the restaurant I was surprised to find my hand on her shoulder, not understanding how this banal gesture was able to fill me with such happiness, such a sense of our having lived through long companionship with one another: I even perceived the rhythm of her breaths, the most intimate meaning of an existence destined from that moment to accompany my own.

"I want to walk," said Marta.

We walked, staying quiet, our steps resounding in nocturnal Rome, and hearing in them the fading away inside us of unspoken words, words it was useless to say out loud.

In her beauty there was something, I don't know, so clear and matinal. Nature lavishes such special care upon some women that, in a state of grace, one sees She chose only these features and those shapes to create a subtle play of contrasting attractions. In Marta, great freedom and sweetness prevailed. Sometimes she thought of something far away from me and was distracted, fleetingly.

It's important to be aware that you are leading someone by the hand, someone who wants to be led. Yet we were walking through those same streets now, and now we were two presences wandering in their separate solitudes, distant, closed in the improbable, trusting only the sound of steps, the pauses . . . That first night it was so lovely to walk together, anywhere, laughing, stopping in front of shops closed up behind their iron screens, with Marta delighted by the jewelers' displays, not worrying about saying anything important, letting ourselves improvise a childish hilarity.

Our hands once more became the hands of teenagers: in their desire for contact, in the way they brought each other to life.

Suddenly the snow began to fall, sparsely.

We went on, street after street, deeply breathing in the perfume of the snow that was invading the deserted city, and Marta was happy as a child, letting the uncertain flakes float against her. She leaned against a wall, looking high up:

"Let's go to your house and make love."

She proposed this in simple gladness, without the feints or automatic anxiety with which women usually offer themselves.

. . . now too the snow is falling, lightly, while she follows me, while I let her follow me. I was listening hard, fearing that from one moment to the next her steps might disappear. Instead they came on steadily, keeping the same distance. We both understood that we could speak through our footsteps; exchanging, in that way, all the questions and all the answers that for two years we had kept silently inside:

"Why did it happen?"

"We've asked ourselves that an infinity of times. The end has its own rules, and sometimes they're just inscrutable."

"It was your nerves, Marta. The scenes you made for no reason, over nothing. Your not understanding . . ."

"No, it was you who never understood."

I lengthened my stride, to slow us down. It was a way of varying the discourse.

"Have you made a new life for yourself?"

"Have you?"

"There you go: do you have to answer every question with a question?"

"Only when your questions come out of your own egotism. When you don't understand that other people have the same rights as you, more rights than you, because sometimes you give the impression of wanting to destroy whatever you hold in your hands. So you can be alone, like a stray dog. Look at you."

I looked at myself in a shop window.

"What about you, Marta, aren't you lonely as a dog? . . . You're wrong about me, that's so typical. Certain women don't understand when a man has so much love for them that they blur into his own crises, his own fear of fate, until his own body takes on all the shadings of a soul . . . And he can't let there be such confusion . . . That's what you didn't understand."

"Maybe it's true. Maybe I can understand it now."

"But now it's late. Don't you hear that bell in the night? It's tolling for us, it's telling us it's *late*."

"I hear it, yes."

"I'd like to turn around, Marta, I'd like to see what marks these years have left on your face. I'd like to know that your face is more relaxed now, and that you don't still go crazy over nothing. . . ."

"I'm looking at your shoulders. I'm trying to read your new life there . . . it's too hard. Your hair is thinner."

Only the empty night could read us completely, with a loving look at our two lives. Perhaps because our lives are, themselves, two nights in love with their own solitude.

. . . I came through the door of what used to be our house, leaving it open. I went up the stairs. I stopped on the landing of the second floor, in front of the door, our door.

Marta's steps, after a hesitation, came in the downstairs door, too. My heart was beating hard: would she keep coming toward me? Would I hear her walking up the stairs?

I moved toward the threshold, stamping my feet to make more noise in the silent building. It was as though these were the last words in our conversation:

"It's after midnight, Marta. Today's my birthday . . . Why have you stopped? Even if you don't want to say happy birthday, at least say something. . . ."

Only her immobility answered me.

"These years . . . seem like a mountain to me. Even our old cat went away, there's nothing, no one waiting for me inside the door anymore. And everything is really ending, even things outside of us. Perhaps these footsteps of ours which aren't going any further, really are our last farewell."

I heard Marta's steps turn back toward the *portone* and fade away in the night already white with snow. I came into the apartment, I didn't turn on the light, I remained standing in the whiteness that outlined everything. Words came back to me:

"Let's go to your house and make love."

I saw again the acts of that love, in every last detail. As if I were living them.

MECCANO-WOMEN

Meccano: children's toy made of pieces of metal that can be dismantled, with which various mechanical constructions can be contrived.

. . . mythology had its own devices and demonized them as monsters: minotaurs, dragons, harpies, chimeras.

"Monsters are less rare than miracles," Balzac insists. And Buffon, who sought to classify them, adds: "The monster is a biological warning which reminds us that nature, even in the guise of sex, is capable of chilling our soul and our desires."

We are living in a time of glut, of dull habituation.

Television, for example, exerts on us a kind of purging of the senses, dosing us over lunch and dinner with every kind of monstrosity that emerges from quotidian news stories or the crimes of history. Finally we feed upon horrors, finding them all alike, unable to differentiate between interpretation and opinion, so that the atrocities of Piazzale Loreto have exactly the same value as massacres by the mafia and the camorra; and the slaughters of Bosnia and Rwanda become equivalent to some hypothetical Lorena Bobbit who chops her unfortunate spouse live in prime time.

The effect of habituation is itself horror. Spectators have become indifferent voyeurs at a massacre. No longer is there indignation or pity, only curiosity streaked with the most morbid cognitive ambition.

Aristotle affirmed: "Monstrosity is not against nature, but against that which should take place in nature."

The Meccano-Women take shape from these considerations. They are simultaneously actresses and bored spectators of themselves. No fresh-faced dollies these, but head toys, careful to keep up appearances as they play their bourgeois social rôles, passing from one man to another in wary secrecy, giving themselves to a different man almost daily. The dual conscience of some women is an old story: the "respectable" one for everyday use, the other dedicated uniquely to squalid coition. However, nothing is ever said openly about these automata, only faint whisperings behind an omertà that is itself middle-class: they'll do it with anyone, they give it to anybody.

Since these women have a dark phallic magnet where their hearts should be, they are drawn by a man's crudest attractions: coarse beauty, youth, bestial endowments, ignorance too; and so they are easily charmed by superficial attentions from men of the crazy-macho type, no less monstrous than themselves, practitioners of obtuse and indiscriminate coitus. Very often it's hints from her meccano-friends that push her toward him: "He's great in bed." And if it's a flop, a phallic failure . . . ?

Painful priestesses of other people's wretched yearnings, sordid orphans of Eros, who punishes them, they anxiously seek an impossible father within the limits of "local pleasure," in the gymnastics of coupling, in which they may be technically but not sensually expert (a prowess that no real and honest professional prostitute would ever boast of). They think that it's they who are controlling the game; they don't understand that their meccano aspect, so fragmented and so dead, can only mean absolute servility.

The mechanism that moves them, in fact, soaked with obscure complexes and thwarted ambitions, goes back to the little horrors of primordial inhumanity. Like third-rate strolling players they rehearse the usual pantomime: they must endure fusion with male bodies which are more and more often those of strangers, offer themselves to be penetrated by these strangers' phalli, by whom they are called upon to celebrate, in a bed, ceremonies which although often hasty, still remain compulsory and squalid rites of idolatry.

The sequence of this pantomime in which she is subjected to the most humiliating experiences unfolds with the contrived and macabre furtiveness of a hired gun accomplishing his hits: the reciprocal undressing, the forced kisses at the beginning, the phallus which has to be gratified, excited, by fingering, by oral coitus. Meccano-Women have as parameters the great phalloi from which there spurts forth no erotic magnetism. A plunge, and then the male asks, idiotically, "Did I hurt you?"

In these cases, coitus is repellent.

It's disturbing to imagine these female bodies, their fragility over-whelmed before masculine anatomic energy. These women, knees planted on the bed, head forced downward as if awaiting decapita-tion. One asks how they manage to absorb it all, with what degree of dilation, I don't speak of their orifices but of their consciences. How do they manage to bear the athletic burden without being broken to bits?

And then the taking in, from time to time, of sperm which is ex-traneous to every tenet of love. To be filled with it, and then get up, go into the bathroom, clean off everything but her dignity, come back to lie down casually in sheets whose stains are the traces of a monstrous act which has become palpable; clean herself again, dry off, still hoping for a profound and impossible orgasm, and then the pauses in which they smoke a cigarette, exchange empty and absurd words, and then begin again. The program, the machine switched on:

"Like this. Bend over."

The stupidity of the male who thinks he's passed some kind of test: "Did you like that? Was it good?"

Her usual response, feigned, hypocritical, tired of all meccano-fe-male hypocrisy: "The best."

Chronic nymphomaniacs afflicted with *libido insatiata?* No, just drifters borne by pathological loneliness, by a thirst for affirmation not satisfied elsewhere, by feminine haughtiness. If you interrogate them confidentially, you learn that they are hiding a profound and bewildered loss whose reasons they don't know, a repugnance for themselves which they will never admit; they offer vague and con-fused justifications. Even if there is truth in what they say they're seeking in the fullness of pleasure, it's something hard to find: the right man. The most embittered may admit, "I'm everything I never wanted to be. And the most humiliating thing is that I've given up so much that's me, for other people's enjoyment."

Their tic which comes from being impotent with Eros can only be cured by an authentic love.

Monstrosity is nostalgia, horrendous and translated into horror, for something unknown, something grand and dramatic which probably filled with its powers the very origins of individual life. It is this nostalgia of not knowing which leads to couplings that become interchangeable, like the horrors that the world of images brings to us each day. All that's left to do is compute the number of phalluses consumed.

EROS AS DEVOTION

This was a story that Parma talked about for years. Speculating. Equivocating.

Luisa Canale had married Gabriele Barilli. She had chosen Gabriele and not Guido Carra, who had accepted her decision to refuse him by behaving absolutely contrary to any logic. Gently, he had blocked the movement of his memories and feelings just as a clock can be stopped, its hands marking the last hour of a time when one was happy, aware that it would be futile to move through the hours and minutes of the future, because the future no longer contained time for him, it was over. It happens. Death can intervene, even though it may not be a physical death: it's just the body going on.

Guido, like Luisa, had made a decision.

He would never be separated from the woman he loved. Now he

lived in a house directly across from the one where she and Gabriele had gone to live after the wedding. Only a garden plot lay between them. And so Luisa and Gabriele would always have that discreet and silent witness, who seemed happy to be seen by them at any moment of the day, just as their life as a couple was seen by him.

He would miss nothing: of their loving, having children, despairs, hopes. And nothing of Guido would be lost on the two of them: he would never love again, never have children, never have hopes; but neither would he know despair. He was content to be like the ivy growing on a wall, a geranium blooming alone, a rainspout: all the meaningless things that, as time passes, become indispensably part of daily life.

Thus it happened that one night Gabriele woke Luisa. She saw him standing by the bed and she asked him anxiously, "Has he done something crazy?" Gabriele smiled at her and answered, "He's doing it now. But it's quiet craziness. Beautiful craziness. Nothing to worry about." They went to the window and watched him.

Guido was bent over the earth in the garden, where he had built a shelter of reeds to protect certain plants from the sun and rain. He was admired throughout the city as a gardener, one who knew every agrarian rite, every ritual of the sun. They could see his shaven head; he had shaved it when Luisa left him to marry another man. A woolen scarf was tied around it.

Luisa asked, "But what's he doing?"

"Hoeing!" answered Gabriele.

"But that's impossible, it's the middle of the night. . . ." Luisa sounded distressed.

"No, I tell you he's hoeing the garden. Can't you see him? He came out an hour ago and first he cut the deadwood out of the climbing rose."

"But why?"

"God knows. But only Guido knows the secrets of the seasons."

They were looking at the sky and mistook the first streak of dawn light for a hint of fair weather. Guido kept working back and forth between the two façades and now Luisa could see the hoe's blade shining; from the flash as it went up and down in the clods, she could tell that it was moving in a joyous rhythm. She thought she could see the man waving his arms as if to send a warning signal to the ghosts of the air, who surely knew that the weed called *Maria Louisa*, and the violets dear to the same Duchess, the violets that the residents of Parma still carry to her tomb in the Capuchin crypt, are born in fragrance only out of soil that has been broken away from where it touches hidden frost.

Gabriele and Luisa would hide and reappear at the window as Guido came closer or went to the other side, and with their eyes they asked each other why he was digging up the garden at daybreak with such energy.

From behind the willow tree they heard a whistle.

"Is he doing that?" whispered Luisa.

Gabriele listened: "Sounds like a bird."

But it was Guido. He reappeared, his lips moving, whistling bird calls, and he left the hoe stuck in a root. He knelt down and lovingly extracted a bulb the size of an egg. He breathed in its odor as if it were a treasure he had discovered. Then he lifted it in his clasped hands, holding it high, and went to sit on the bench, arranging his cloak around him. His dog came to thrust his nose between Guido's knees, and Guido scrutinized the thickness of the clouds and the sharpness of the first icy light.

That light fell on the bulb, illuminating it.

≈

"Look. It's snowing!" cried Gabriele.

The wind twisted the falling snow against the peripheral

glimpses of Parma, the windows of the surrounding façades, the branches of the highest trees; but there under the garden wall the wind could not pass, so the snow kept falling on Guido and the dog, his unique friend, with a discreet and enfolding softness.

Guido let it fall over him, unmoving, smiling at the dog or to himself, but most of all at the bulb, which he lifted up again to show off, pale and cold, and yet the growing light caressed it, slowly sending golden reflections over it.

"What's he doing? Why doesn't he go inside?" sighed Luisa when she saw Guido and his dog all white with snow.

"Let him alone. He's happy."

And in fact he was. Happy to show Luisa and Gabriele his own heart, as if it had been dug out of his rib cage and enclosed in the bulb which gave off, now and then, a flash of gold. A human heart that had been frozen but which still knew how to respond, with a tiny halo of enchantment, to the pity of an endless winter sky.

Luisa and Gabriele understood perfectly that Guido was holding his heart in his joined hands. But they didn't say it. And into their hearts too there penetrated a sharp pain, cold as snow.

Gabriele closed the interior shutters over the windows, protecting Luisa's modesty as she came close to him and took him in her arms, creating two figures which could come together now in sleep. And Guido was imagining this moment, because he had never left them, even if he had never lifted his head to see if Gabriele and Luisa were really there behind the window.

"Come back to bed?" asked Gabriele.

Luisa crossed the room and lay down beside him. They conjoined in love, and to Gabriele it seemed that he was making love for Guido, too, as if the heat of his own blood could warm the frozen bulb that he felt now inside his breast.

They drifted into sleep with the certainty that the three of them would never be separated, and in this certainty they clung to each other's hands. Before he fell asleep Gabriele thought, "We haven't had children yet. But even if we never can. . . ."

There was Guido, down there, sitting unmoving under the snow. Guido, who was sensing that very thought.

EROS AND PLAY

Sometimes the child Eros of the antique myths comes back to play with R. and me.

Blindfolded Eros, with his diaphanous wings. Being a child, he loved to play, and only while he played was his blindfold removed. Our games begin after a series of sexual acts which may be exhausting, but which do not consume our reciprocal desire to keep on possessing one another. How? Through playfulness, of course. Our bodies find ways of embracing, of mingling; we give new names to gestures and caresses with the silly sweetness only childhood knows.

Eros has helped us know that we are profoundly alive. What happiness that he returns to us now with all the knowing ingenuousness of children's games wherein we first tasted the truth of life, the first analogies between dream and reality. . . .

It's impossible to explain to phallic idiots in what, for example, the pleasures of a *covina* consist. They'd think we were crazy. Their penetrations are obtuse, untouched by playfulness or fantasy. No, it's not worth trying to explain *covina* to them. So let the word remain as it is, like the enigmatic contents of that box the protagonist receives and the spectator cannot see in the final moments of Buñuel's *Belle de Jour*. And Séverine, played by Catherine Deneuve, becomes illuminated.

Even the name by which I call R. — *Donnino* — becomes part of our game, which is the opposite of the violence that kills Eros. Of course the woman player needs to have, as R. does, a sensual intelligence which, having gone beyond the hidden anxieties of predictable sexual performance, enhances Eros much as the meadow and the sky set off a soaring kite. R. and I have flown our kites together. And the coded language of the game that makes each the other's accomplice belongs only to us.

A deep gratitude grows in us toward the one who bestows this privilege upon us: to understand each other, to be sexually alike, down to the most fugitive shadings.

One comes back to the concept of music. Eros' jocosity is the "counterpoint" which, as its texts instruct us, allows the *appoggiatura*, commonly explained by orchestral players as the "reciprocal sustaining of clandestine notes." These clandestine notes, with their lightness and humor, linger in the heart's memory more durably than the great concerto of the act of love itself.

Then R. and I fall asleep, arranging our bodies in the perfect position I've already described; understanding that a man can clasp a woman around her waist and in so doing console her, console himself as well, for the memory of the times each of them has had to be alone, clasping only herself, himself, in a bed with no companion or with the wrong one, yet imagining that one's desolation was shared by an invisible, complicit, perfect presence.

Holding each other like this we can bear the immense flight into unknowable eternity, into mystery.

We sleep, breathing in time with each other, often dreaming the same dream. In the morning we awaken with regret: the sleep of the child Eros dissolves with the first ray of sunlight through a crack in the shutters, like a butterfly flying away.

"Loyalty in love is beautiful."

"It's a new language we've learned together. I love speaking it with you."

"It was already inside us in darkness, silent and unuttered."

"When we speak it, we're showing gratitude and respect for our life which we've hurt so often by our own mistakes . . ."

The winter light is blue and violet. It is part of the serenity in which we separate, to spend the day apart, knowing we are loyal to one another.

"Loyalty is different from fidelity. It exists out of conviction, not duty."

It is the most precious quality of life.

I tell R. how loyalty prevents little catastrophes, and how the little catastrophes in a relationship are like the sturgeon which the Po in flood flung up, making it describe a long arc against the sky, and the sturgeon fell like a meteor in front of us, between the half-toppled houses. It gave a final swipe of its tail, knocking over a young tree, and then lay stiff and still. It weighed more than a hundred kilos, and it would have been the most beautiful sturgeon anyone had ever seen, except that it was covered head to tail with a layer of slime already hard as stone. And if the flood hadn't left a terrifying wound along one side.

I kept on staring at the sturgeon, overcome by grief that left me unable to speak, that made me touch its scales lightly with my fingertips.

"Loyalty saves us from this," I tell R. "It keeps love from the worst ending, from the death of the sturgeon."

Solitary, saturnine lust. Here in Parma they call it *Bramosa di te stesso*, a solo for your own willing hand.

It can begin with some mild irritation. Because suddenly you see, just for an instant, a naked girl behind a window of the house across the way. She's pulling on her pants with a quick gesture in which you read the habits of her whole life, and then she disappears, and everything starts to happen as it does to the mad lover of the Po who wanders, whistling, between the delta and the sea, dreaming of palest blue artemisia, of viburnum blossoms, clusters of water-birds whose flesh is bitter, and then all at once it comes: the mirage, the flash of the red heron in the deep violet of the sky.

Or else you're there, sitting among the loafers at the Blue Bar, leaning back in the wicker chair, staring at clouds of sparrows, waiting for sundown, savoring it like a ripe apricot melting slowly in the mouth.

They're sitting outside and they feel good, with their secret longing for women, as if they were all under the same sheet — so they say — and in the air you can feel *al mai po'*, the nevermore, the women you can never again hope to have, a presentiment of the end, and because of this they talk boastfully, using *paroli zo'd'pòst*, crazy words, *da putlètt*, baby words, and for these reasons full of beauty and sweetness: their *bablare*, their big talk, is without meaning. And suddenly one may say, surprisingly:

"Know something? I talk to God like that, too, *come as méta la lengua in boca a na dòna*." Like putting my tongue in a woman's mouth.

And now, in that special moment, a girl is passing by, one who gives off the idea of going home to happiness, moving her majestic haunches, cunningly calculating her stride, the walk of a woman of Parma, just for them, just for the idlers in the Blue Bar. Stendhal is supposed to have said, "If a foreigner were to ask me what is the face of Parma, I would say that it is grace itself. It's the face of one of that city's women, her face and her walk. The city was created for her . . ."

The loungers get up, shaking off their laziness with a gesture of their arms, trying to look casual, and each wanders off, going his own way, following that swaying walk. The white wicker chairs are deserted.

Then the lonely lust explodes inside you like the storms of summer in these parts, when you see the first big drops imprint themselves, fuming, on the barnyard dust, clanging like coins. One of those storms is coming, the kind that slashes the curtains of the sky, and here the throng of swallows flees off into the clouds, over there a waspish swarm of shrilling people rushes to shelter under the archways. A smell of rain-soaked dust and lightning rises, taking your breath away, making you dizzy. And then you remember the odors that made up part of your childhood.

In the fields, the *contadini* lift pitchforks full of hay and hold them over their heads like umbrellas to shelter from the rain, between thunderbolts.

Anyway, this is how your smoldering lust ignites inside you, and you carry it home, you lie down with it on the bed and there you make love to yourself . . . A flavor that's unusually intense, almost as if it were your soul that's giving it off, bitter and sweet at the same time, becomes concrete, physical: it insinuates itself down there, still keeping a special lightness. This is not simple masturbation, it's much more: it's as though you were telling a story of pure eroticism to yourself alone, a picaresque and amiable tale, in which the very weight of flesh transforms itself to radiance.

I believe that the same thing happens to a woman when in this condition she makes love alone in her bed.

You touch your body. A subtle and delicate energy guides your movements, it's as if your fingers were running over the keyboard of priceless pleasure, with an enormous yearning to return into your very self, and at the same time, the desire for an unknown elsewhere. You find yourself a boy, a girl, once more, with simple fantasies that follow one after the other, just as in a time when the world had not yet done anything to you. The exuberant flowering of these thoughts and images warms you, they're like long-ago embers, their fragrance drifting from the fireplace. . . . There, you're devising perfect couplings out of these images, and amorous games like a delicious music, and you remember that the first love-play of your life smelled of clean laundry.

Whom would you like to have there in your bed?

Everyone and no one.

You re-enter honestly into the deepest part of yourself. The gestures you repeat take on mysterious forms. It's almost as if we were speaking with the intact verity of our own sex, taking up a conversation that had been interrupted, it now seems, by the interference of others.

In those gestures, while you caress yourself and find again those places no stranger can discover, like making a cone-shaped incision in a watermelon to see how red and ripe it is, Eros presides with particular splendor, because he is content with you, with you alone, he's your dearest friend, you need no other, it's as though he were seated on the edge of your bed and smiling at you, with *a company smile*, as they say in my country. An Eros with perfect pitch in this duet for a single voice.

It's Eros as ventriloquist: he speaks to you, but it's you who lend him voice.

You feel him in your fingertips, like violin strings, and in your solo a thousand duets resonate; you're incarnated in your wild imaginings. You understand that Eros lives in spite of the love you make with others, but in respect of it, too. Eros, my soul, which touches all that's desirable. . . . And guided by that friend, you desire yourself, longingly you desire yourself, you are happily forced to desire yourself — what a luminous miracle! — until you are overcome by that tiredness which even life itself endures, and when life no longer desires itself (it's not your desire for life that counts here) then, only then, it's over. . . .

My cat Gina jumps onto the bed, curls herself on my stomach, wanting to become my furry paunch.

I turn my head, and it seems that even the geranium, nodding alone on the balcony, is drunk with a celestial *Bramosa* that enfolds it; that there exists an Eros-ventriloquist for every living thing.

THE EROS OF SUDDEN REMEMBRANCE

Marco is making love, serenely, with a compliant girlfriend, and another friend looks on, pleased by their quiet happiness, and his girlfriend too . . . But then, into this apparent serenity comes the need for things to be in order, for bodies that really move in harmony with their desires, deep as knowledge; a longing for silence, for the quiet night, where it's possible to smell the perfume of the linden trees through open windows, where silence, like a sea, has a distant backwash of joyous songs. . . .

Marco suddenly pulls away; it's almost as if a lightning flash had blazed out of the ephemeral serenity of their bodies. He withdraws from his partner, leaving not only her body but also the complicity that was supposed to unite him with the other lovers. He rolls up in a corner of the bed, like a wounded dog at the edge of a road, and takes no further part; it's as if he no longer sees the bodies, the room.

Marco stares at the dark. Marco is the dark.

The others watch him, frightened. . . .

⁂

And now the friends are outside in the night, walking, true friends together, and their bodies breathe that friendship, purified by the sudden memory that took hold of Marco. They are forgetting the acts that, a little while ago, brought them so meaninglessly together, or perhaps now they know they've misunderstood something, a shame that was nothing but sick solitude. The friends understand that even serenity can be misunderstood, that a sickness that possesses us can turn itself into a calm that is its own opposite.

Marco and one of the young women lift their heads and look at a star, and maybe they think that what they see up there is, in any case, a god.

On the banquet table, red in the moonlight, are the year's first watermelons. The friends keep walking back and forth, sinking their faces into the red slices. And Marco is startled at the tears in his eyes: who will ever really love him, in a future that's supposed to be so near? And will there still be someone who will want and who will know how to love him, really, with a clean heart, without having been a victim of a sexuality that belongs nowhere except here, in his own waste land?

What Marco remembered: suddenly he saw his mother again, in a fragment of night, after a violent argument with his father about Malo, whom she knew to be his lover, the cause of her distress: his mother moaning "Malo, Malo, Malo," in an obsessive refrain, leaning against the oval mirror beside the bed, alone, naked, bent over herself . . . The child Marco, watching from the door, thought she had become smaller, shrunken by the anguish that gripped her, and now she was doing something with her fingers between her thighs, some gesture that went faster and faster, accompanied by a singsong lament of rage and profanity, to forget Malo and evoke her, too, a haste like desperate sobbing, watching her own gesture in the mirror, as if being able to see it made it less crazy, calling her eyes to witness (like the child witness, Marco, forcing himself not to run away).

His mother stabbed her fingers ever more deeply inside, her head went back and forth as if she were denying something, until her desperation ended in an orgasm. Then she fell on her knees under the holy image on the wall, a painting of the Madonna and Child: "Fuck sex!" she shouted, weeping, "Fuck love!"

She lay at the base of the wall as if she were dead, and Marco came and crouched beside her, holding her against him, smoothing her hair, begging her: "Come on now. Come on, Mother."

His mother turned toward him, staring at him with glassy eyes that were not seeing him but his father, the traitor husband, who since he had fallen for Malo had never held her in his arms like that.

She murmured, "I love you. I still love you."

Marco understood that these words weren't for him, that he did not exist for that declaration of love, that it was for his father. And so he took his father's place, feeling like a man, a traitor, and not loved for himself. . . . He held his mother more closely and kissed her on the mouth, not a son's kiss but a lover's, wondering how a man kissed. And he said, "I love you too. And it's finished with Malo, Mother. I'm here, just for you."

He began stroking his mother's body, lightly, and again he tried with his entire self to imagine how an adult might caress a woman's flesh. Images, speculations, passed through him. With great delicacy he touched the place out of which he had been born, and it seemed natural to do it with the grace that she, his mother, had sent into his blood as she created him; the greatest of all the gifts she could pass on to him.

They both noticed the same thing in the same instant. The painting above them, the Madonna and the Child. And it was as if the light of purity came down upon them, enfolding them as they stayed clasped in their embrace.

And that was the strength they needed to compose themselves back into their usual roles again, lucidly remembering regret and remorse, but also the dignity of existence. What was left over was concentrated into a subtle dissolution of every instinct that lets us communicate in consonance with those like ourselves.

FROM THE NOTEBOOK OF PASSING DAYS

Eros and mauve.

I am reading in time, with the sentiment of time that suddenly takes hold of us, the desire to be sought out, just as one seeks the traces of lost loves, in places that have watched us live, even for brief periods.

I think about something Proust confessed: "The name of Parma, one of the cities I most desired to visit after having read *The Charterhouse*, seemed compact, smooth, mauve-colored, sweet. . . ."

There exists an Eros that has no need of corporeal union; diffuse, waiting to be breathed in like a breeze, to be watched, like an oblique ray of sunlight.

It is breathed and it is contemplated in certain places, it is *of* these places: certain half-illuminated piazzas, half in shadow, certain sidestreets, or a row of archways in a frank April morning.

I call it "mauve-colored" Eros.

Someone I don't know has started coming into my house.

A girl, I think.

I really don't know who it is. It would be easy for many people to get a copy of my keys. The intruder is very clever at slipping into these rooms when I'm absent. Clearly, she is watching me.

I'm doing nothing to discover her identity.

If this is a game for her, it's one for me, too. I like that: the little mystery of her visiting me when I'm not here, the ways she finds to animate my absence.

She leaves notes for me, casually, on the furniture, in an obviously disguised handwriting so that I won't recognize it. I read, "Let's sleep together tonight."

But then she doesn't come. I no longer believe that she will keep the appointments she announces. I know she won't come.

Here and there she leaves me odd presents. Hung on the wall of the study, for example, a big framed photograph in which there appear the candid dome of a temple, a stretch of meadow, and the walls of Katmandu. Or a bizarre bowler hat, with a magician's wand, arranged on an armchair.

Her takeover of my house is progressing. I open a closet and find, among my suits, her elegant evening gown. Or I pull open a drawer, and there are brightly colored tee shirts with extravagant graphics and slogans in different languages: some invite me to meditation, others to supreme erotic effort.

I wonder if one day I'll learn who she is, this artful tease whose games awaken in me the Eros of curiosity.

❧

It bothers me to read the stories about "moral transgressions of the masses" which are invading the newspapers. Headlines like, "What's *Your* Vice?," "Better Perverse Than Indifferent," "Lolita in

Manhattan . . . and Elsewhere" . . .

Every time, I think of Nino.

He used to say, "Against vulgarity, it's important to recognize the good inside each mystery." The words of the *Blue Mazurka* say this too, calling the moon *pendula alma*, a wandering soul, and at the *Merlin Cocai*, a nightclub on the Po, Nino himself, all sleaze and flash in his flame-red jacket, would give the downbeat.

And then my soul stopped wandering like the moon.

I read the newspaper's garish coverage of yet another pronouncement from the Pope, this time to the Cairo Conference on population and development:

"Holy Father Says Sex Not Taboo."

I lift up my eyes.

It looks like the lunar surface, but it's really a complex of DNA and protein photographed through an electron microscope. The enlargement is leaning against the wall of my room and it sends out an echo from the abysses sunken in the secret of the human body, a kind of celestial vault turned upside down. Instead of calling it the genetic code, it ought to be seen as the musical score of nature: exactly as the dot and the dash used for the Morse code represent the letters of the alphabet. Thus in this huge enlargement I recognize the sacred language that brought us into being.

It is as though I were listening to my own interior, where there exists a language that we *are*, mirroring the vastness of the cosmos. And even if we can grasp only the visible, unbounded silences of this language, I know that it communicates and speaks, while the other words I generally make use of — from my mind, from my heart — seem lifeless to me.

I can feel words insinuating themselves into me, words that reach me from the nucleus of mystery and that console my spirit, sweeten my loneliness.

My father died a few months ago.

His death keeps growing in me, like a blade which at the beginning barely pricked my skin but now is cutting slowly, slowly through flesh and bone.

One day, my father explained to me in his own simple words, and so unexpectedly as to leave me mute with wonder, that which I mean by Eros. He said, "It's like the flight of a butterfly." Thinking of my father, yesterday, strangely, I wrote some lines for my mother who is alive and well. I wonder why the heartbreak over my father's death was transferred to her:

> Your mother's life goes on
> in the stockings she hung up to dry.
> Days later, after she's dead,
> nobody remembers the clothesline.
> Your touch profanes her toothbrush
> and you start to pray for her,
> for the grace to keep believing
> in her loose tooth.
> She found a way to leave.
> Living with habits she has willed to you,
> your eyes cloud over, you can't see.

CURIOUSER AND CURIOUSER

There are some women — like M. — in whom Eros is unleashed only after furious fights.

The destruction began.

The door slammed, making the Hebrew lamps tremble.

The knight on the rearing horse, by Baron Sorghental, now had good reason to rear. The oval plates from the hills of Bassano, painted with musical instruments and notes, confronted M., tinkling like little mandolins.

They paid dearly, the largest one plummeted to rest with a gaping hole like a lost eye, rather like Marshal Niepperg after some daunting battle. On the plate glass table in the living room, books, magazines, and piles of mail were swept to the floor and the little Swiss monkey began madly polishing the tin shoe he held in one paw, shrugging intermittently.

The Han period Buddha — souvenir of a particularly happy trip I'd made, and M. knew it — fell to the ground, giving new meaning to a passage from the Ramayana: "Smile on, o expiring sage." A few days later, the statue came home again, wounds sutured, from the shop of a restorer friend in Via dei Giubbonari. From the ceramic fragments I carried to him in a cardboard box, he calculated my erotic rush toward the end:

"We're getting there," he said. "They're coming faster now."

The Commodus with the attributes of Hercules, an archaeological rarity, sneered at me; a good sign, I thought, but M. seized him by the attributes and flung him against the wall. I remember that I felt a surge of joy as I hurled a porcelain figurine, a flower girl in a dirndl, against the front door — part of a group M. loved. These Viennese statuettes reminded her of the dances of Fanny Elsser, the notes dear to Anna Strauss.

So I threw a second one, a third. The poor creatures with their round red cheeks lay on the carpet, decimated, and instead of going to the restorer, they ended up in the trash.

The aikiku, the Japanese dagger, another *souvenir de voyage*, made criminal instincts surface. The Peruvian figures, painted with symbols of eternal peace, confirmed that death is not really the worst thing that can happen.

The bacchantes were ripped out of the Aubusson tapestry because they reminded M. of putative fornicatresses.

An incense burner in the form of a deer was smashed to bits: its horns were too long and certainly alluded to something.

≋

As you will have understood, I used to be a collector of precious objects.

Into the Indian vase modelled on a human skull surmounted with a red and yellow duck, M. tried to inculcate the ideas she wasn't able to get into my head, with the result that she found herself wringing the duck's neck while I knelt on the rug, carefully picking up the pieces and putting them into the carton.

I suggested that perhaps she shouldn't break the mirrors. But she's not superstitious, and so up and then down flew the looking glass where I used to find myself when I woke from certain dreams. She did not, however, permit herself any iconoclastic acts — M. is a believer and occasionally a practicing Catholic — and so the Stations of the Cross lampshades were saved in extremis, and the angel ashtrays only rarely took wing.

At last an imperious samurai voice was heard shouting "Enough!" It clanged from the Yokohagi-dogusoku armour. The mouth of its mask gaped wide, between the wings of the helmet forged in the likeness of the mythical Ho-ho bird; the vambraces and gauntlets reached stiffly forward in a minatory gesture.

And then, some last strength, nourished perhaps by our very exhaustion, drove us to the last piece of furniture left intact — the bed, with its brass-trimmed headboard. Its only quality was comfort. M. stretched out across it, subdued now but wildly excited.

I fell beside her. Neither of us was trying to best the other. We both had done that. She lay in the attitude of abandon she liked best, letting me enter her from the side. What link could there be between her readiness to respond so perfectly to my rhythm of cadences and desires, and the hostility she had just displayed?

I even managed to shape a thought: How moral physical beauty can be!

EROS AND LITTLE SUBTERFUGES

Who knows why I'm only now remembering this. Perhaps because, in my dissatisfaction, I'm looking for something with which I can identify.

For a while I used to go with Lydia, a girl who told lies. It wasn't her powers of seduction that charmed me — I really found nothing special about them — but the exquisite pleasure I experienced when I spotted her lies, naked of any refinement or cunning, easy to discover. In them I saw symbolically enclosed the very essence of the feminine Lie, which is a curious piece of clockwork.

I would sit on the edge of the bed when she got up to go to the bathroom. I looked around the room, and, infallibly, there they were: the slippers. Pale blue, huge, men's. They peeped out from unthinkable places, or they would suddenly spring into my view. It was obvious that Lydia had gotten rid of them only at the last possible moment, following her vocation for subterfuge, but without putting any thought into it. They would be leaning against the magazine rack, or between the bottom ledge of the armoire and the floor, or on top of one another on the highest bookshelf . . . if they didn't fall out onto the floor as I looked in the nightstand, when, after not having seen them anyplace else, I would open the door to see them collapse on the floor beside my feet, where they seemed to stretch out and breathe in the beatitude of my grimace.

I used to pick them up, look at them.

I thrust my feet into them, wherein they disappeared. Inside that enormous blue footgear, I imagined a giant shuffling: the abominable snowman, I secretly called the mysterious guest with whom I shared Lydia's free time.

There is a period of lightness, of hidden laughter that inhabits us. Will it come back to me?

EROS' OBSESSIONS AND PERVERSIONS

Definition:

"*Scopophilia*: neologism primarily used in psychoanalysis to define voyeurism. It is motivated by *partial pulsions*, that is, non-specific sexual excitation, and it may comprise part of a preparatory act, known as 'preliminary pleasure,' which serves to increase 'final' pleasure. Only when this preliminary pleasure excludes every other form of sexual activity does scopophilia become a perversion.

"An aberrational need for observation may be associated with scopophilia, as may exhibitionism, which is in certain cases repressive; there is in fact identification between 'inverted' voyeurism, which consists in the exhibition of one's own body, and scopophilia."

I know husbands who get excited watching their own wives being possessed by another man; lovers who are excited when they watch their beloved satisfy another person's every desire. These are abject beings. In their perversions I find only squalor.

Cesare was a watcher, but what he sought might be called "Eros of Darkness": he deserved the pity given to those who risk their lives for some desperate need, knowing every station on the road to Calvary.

He was a gardener, or rather a poet of plants and flowers, who recreated harmony within the beauties created by nature. He was married to Rosa. And Rosa brought her lovers to the house, sleeping with them in the marriage bed. Cesare was exiled to a cot downstairs, and he would even bring their morning coffee to the couple who had sex throughout the night, while he had listened from his cot to his wife's cries of pleasure, the sounds of their lovemaking.

Rosa had made him a slave of her cruelty, the humiliated servant of her carnal caprices, and at a certain point Cesare didn't react any more, giving himself over totally to the morbid pain of being treated like a thing to be destroyed. And so he had begun to flee into the Roman night, to be the watcher of other people's intertwinings: a twisted ransom he paid himself by watching couples whose female partner was not Rosa, the wife he continued to love.

Cesare told me his drama little by little, gaining confidence, winning my friendship. I first came to know him when he had sunk from being a princely gardener held in great respect to occasionally looking after plants at people's houses. He had turned the neglected plants on my terrace into a little paradise.

Cesare liked me. And I came to love him, too. He would have laid down his life for me. He used to come visit me when I was alone and having practical problems, which he then solved for me. His affection for me let him intuit, through some magic of the senses, my difficult moments. Once when I had a high fever he came and sat beside my bed for two days. Nursing me. But most of all watching me, in silence, with an endless kindness in his smile; the kindness that made him capable of making plants and flowers expand in incomparable glory.

Cesare prowled through the night, among the stagnant sumps by the Tiber, through patches of reeds and scrub, along the sticky banks or plunging blindly through tangles of weeds, holding his breath. What he was hunting, all through the tattered edges of Rome, was something disgusting.

His quarry was men and women in coitus. They would see him and he, knowing he was discovered, ran away, head down, through the dark hiding places. The men, alarmed, jumped up. Women detached themselves from their lover's member, crying out their hate.

Someone ran after him, grabbed him. Yanked off his jacket. A storm of blows.

Cesare was bleeding from his nose and mouth. But he didn't care. He went on. Other women with their knees in the mud. Under the very bridges of the city the Roman night was paved with fornications. He flushed out dogs who had curled up under some bush, too ashamed to die out under the clear starry night. Under the bridge of Viale Marconi, he saw no women, only mangy tomcats who yowled as they thrust into stray pussies.

There came a moment in which Cesare was leaning back against a tree, atop a mound of trash, the distant glow of Rome flashing through the leaves. It was as if his look fled backwards out of the surrounding shadows, into the darkness inside his skull. His head bent over his chest, sweat poured down his face. His nails digging into the bark, shoulders shaking, he wept, murmuring, "My God, help me."

One night Cesare managed to spy on a happy couple.

They were making love in a car, without brutality, without any ugliness. She was loving him with such tenderness and grace that Cesare was reminded of his favorite plants when he had helped them to shine more brightly than the surrounding sky.

In the woman he saw Rosa, as he had always hoped she would be with him.

And such was the felicity that these two displayed before his eyes that it entered his heart, he felt it to be his. In a flash he thought it would be a crime to let this happy moment, which had come to him from others, end. He also thought that to kill a man like him would be no crime; it would be liberation.

Thus did my friend Cesare free himself.

Definition:

"*Fetishism*: perversion in which only a single part of the body (hair, breasts, pubic hair, etc.) or a single item of dress (shoes, stockings, underpants, etc.) is capable of awakening sexual appetite. The resulting conflicts manifest themselves in love-related illnesses (*Liebeskrankheit*). Ellis holds that 'There is no part of the human body which may not be erogenous'.

"Most frequent parts: *the hand*, decisive element of sexuality; *feet*, foot fetishism is widely diffused and is complicated by such factors as shoe fetishism; the *pubis*. . . .

"The predisposition to fetishism, like all infantile predispositions, is inevitably doomed to repression and guilt complexes which begin in early childhood."

Mafalda Bordi's body charmed all Parma when she became a mother, and from this beauteous mother was born Pietro's incomprehensible ugliness.

Parma reacted with astonishment and sarcasm. How could Mafalda have given birth to her exact opposite? Pietro grew up despised by everyone, as if being ugly were his fault. As he grew, he was tortured by dreams wherein he was watching himself being born like a twisted stump in an enchanted garden; he saw a freak emerge from a vagina which was a symbol of perfection, created by God with an artist's hand; it was even something he could hear: he himself the only false note in a ravishing score.

And that uterine cavity, admired by a virile throng, became his nightmare even when he was awake. It was there, in his head, like an idol, a gilded door profaned by the unworthy.

Wandering through the city, he felt he recognized his mother's marvellous image in the eyes of all those who looked questioningly at him, or stared at him while they pretended to be looking elsewhere; even in the white pupils of the blind Migliavacca, the Paganini of the Mazurka, who played the violin sitting on the ground like a beggar.

He used to pray: "God, please make me a little bit better looking." Thinking incessantly about Mafalda's admirers, whom he detested, every morning he would pose naked in front of the mirror and force his eyes to begin their long descent along his body in the hope that something beautiful, a mole, anything, might have come to embellish it. It happens even to trees. Some solitary bud. But the tufts and branches of his tree remained inexorably desolate.

But Pietro was as clever and intelligent as he was ugly. He learned to play every instrument so that women who would otherwise have turned their heads the other way began to pay attention to him. He conquered them by his masterful piano playing; touching the violin with the same angelic touch as blind Migliavacca; with his clarinet evoking memories of nymphs and fauns; wringing from the guitar the melodious emotions awakened by a happy love.

He understood very well that women would let themselves be possessed by the harmonies with which he enchanted them, and then he in his turn possessed them, entered into them through the hidden gilded door, using the safe-conduct pass of music as an acceptable pretext, which kept him from ever needing to force his way across any natural threshold as an impostor.

And every time he entered a woman, the aria from *Don Carlo* came to his mind: *"Ella giammai m'amò! . . . Non, quel cuor chiuso e` a me. . . ."* — "She never loved me! No, that heart is closed to me. . . ."

But it was not the voice of his mind that burst into song; it was his wounded soul, left behind, there outside the prodigious vaginal borderland out of which his ill-made body had emerged. And his mother's sex, now immense and astral, shining like a constellation in the vault of heaven, became an eye that watched him, never losing sight of him for an instant, while he exhibited himself — precisely for her to see — in prodigious fornications.

He mustn't disappoint her. In some way he had to make up for the disappointment he had provoked by being born.

And so he — who felt himself to be a born sinner — brought to these acts all the passion appropriate to reprobates in quest of redemption. Thus it was that his intelligence, which might itself have been defined as genital, and the knowing constancy with which he managed to sustain pleasure in women, combined to nourish an amatory art rich in unthinkable erotic refinements.

Pietro created himself as a great lover, and, at a certain point, it didn't matter to many women that he was ugly, so very ugly. There exist, by the grace of God, females of the human species who are not about to cavil much about the looks of the person who gives them such incredible pleasure.

But his obsession remained his mother's golden door, like the grimace of a god before whom, at the end of each session of lovemaking which left his partner blissfully exhausted, he performed a genuflection, glad to receive some sign of approval; happy if the idol were to say to him, "Bravo, you've done it again," even if it were in the wrong time and place.

And after each success, he felt the obligation and the voluptuous need to carry a bit of evidence off with him. Like the skilled lion-hunter who brings home the mane of the king of the forest. The sexual acts concluded, Pietro would accomplish yet another, for himself. Kneeling on the bed, he indeed genuflected between the woman's sprawled legs, before her door which remained ajar after such avidity. He placed a kiss there, in truth one that was not entirely amorous, since each woman responded with a little shriek of pain.

Pietro, once more with practiced art, had pulled out a tiny tuft of pubic hair with his teeth. The tired woman thought this was some ulterior erotic caprice. But it was something else. It was as though he were setting a sacred seal there, authenticating the ransom he had paid. Pietro kept each tuft in a carefully folded sheet of paper, writing the name and surname of the woman, the date, and a brief comment, such as: "Exceptional" (the adjective was followed by + whose number indicated the degree of intensity), "She told me 'You are the only one. I've never felt anything like this before.'"

The folded papers grew into piles over the years.

From time to time Pietro would consult them, looking upwards to where Mafalda, long dead, still watched him from her skies, murmuring, "Do you see, Mother? Are you pleased with me?"

But there came the time that comes to all of us. When our decline approaches, and our human forces begin to weaken, and the skills we brought to music are thwarted by our own fingers. It may happen that even a great artist, growing old, begins to fumble and to fail.

Pietro understood what he must do.

Unfolding all those slips of paper was like reliving the happy episodes of life, and every woman's name, every date, stabbed his heart. He saw again forgotten faces, he remembered circumstances with perfect clarity, living them again. He gathered up the tufts of pubic hair and felt them warm the hollow of his hand, as if they were soft feathers that had once enclosed a fowl's beatitude.

His hands filled with these relics, he went out on the terrace. He who knew how to play all the instruments of the orchestra now seemed to be conducting one. Arms flung out, leaning forward, he opened his fingers, closing his eyes so that he wouldn't see, until he felt his hands empty once more. Only then did he look again.

The tufts which had belonged to so many women, which Pietro had ripped out at the height of their moments of glorious delight, were dispersed now, floating through the air, and the sun had wrapped them in a ray of light, and then a little whirlwind lifted them, scattering them up, up, so high. . . .

There where his mother's gilded door no longer was — to Pietro's farewell glance — a pitiless eye. It was now, finally, something gentle, something forgiving, and Pietro identified himself in a new conjunction of a son's body and a mother's, and in his own body he saw the beauty of the deer who, as he moves, knows that the hunter is waiting, and with him an inescapable destiny; the deer who, aware these are his last steps, executes them with supreme regality.

Pietro heard distinctly the voice of his mother Mafalda Bordi, it too dissolved into the impalpable consistence of the universe, where there is perhaps no distinction between beauty and ugliness. And her voice was inviting him, lovingly: "Now you can come back inside me, my son. Yes, now at last the great door is truly golden, and crossing its threshold no longer disappoints anyone . . . You don't need to prove anything anymore."

This happened to Pietro Bordi, about whom various psychiatrists and social assistants had written reports:

" . . . profession: one-man band. Sex maniac. Fetishist with obvious degenerative signs. Case interesting for paradoxical grace with which subject endures an obsessive neurosis, a compulsion to repeated genital stimulation. Subject should however be kept under strict observation . . . perhaps by a maternal eye."

⁂

Definition:

"*Zoöerastia*: neologism created by Krafft-Ebing to distinguish from *bestiality* those cases in which the sexual act practiced upon animals has pathological origins and thus is dependent on hereditary defects, constitutional neurosis, on a kind of impulse to perform an act against nature, and, more generally, on some grave defect of heterosexuality."

⁂

Until a few years ago, in the Lombardi Museum in Parma — dedicated to the memory and relics of Maria Louisa of Hapsburg, ruler of our city, who made her solemn entry into the Dukedom on April 19, 1816 — four golden rings could be seen if one looked for them on a wall that was discreetly around a corner.

These rings have disappeared since I first wrote about them, reflecting on their history. There is a troubling story about them, the affair of Maria Louisa and the horse Alexandre.

The President of Internal Affairs at the time denounced as slanderous certain political documents which, however, nothing proves to have been apocryphal; among them a confidential account written by the Chief Secretary of the Division of Justice and Good Government to Count Adam von Neipperg:

". . . At seven o'clock in the evening I arrived at the Menagerie as you ordered, and I saw: I fulfilled the thankless task, observed all that there was to observe, with words I would wish not to be mine I describe such a spectacle as to freeze up every Christian soul, and so saddened am I to name Our August Sovereign that herein I permit myself to indicate her as *Herself* . . . The act of bestiality between *Herself* and the filthy animal, and I impart this with total bewilderment in my heart, this act was accomplished before my very eyes, which I wished blind. . . ."

Filthy, perhaps, but Alexandre the Horse was a magnificent example of his species. A popular song of that time, written in dialect so dense as to require something akin to cryptanalysis, can be translated into the following acts:

". . . The Duchess came to the Woods. Afterwards the Superintendent of Her Majesty's Forests and Menageries gave severe orders to keep all the hunters and intruders away. In the Gelsi Menagerie, there was light in Alexandre's stable, and the Keeper cleared the way.

"The Duchess went into the stable and closed the door behind her. She liked seeing the traces of ancient peasant life on the walls. She had kept them from taking down a Christ painted with adoring blasphemy as a poor unhappy cripple; but he had been moved behind a pillar so that his eyes under the crown of thorns could not see. Alexandre greeted her, stamping his hoof. There was fresh straw neatly arranged; she stepped out of her shoes, feeling how warm and smooth the bricks were; well-being came up into her from her bare soles.

"Her happiest moment was in those steps. The two came closer to each other, like a girl meeting her friend in a deserted street, feeling a first, happily troubled perplexity. Alexandre's eyes grew larger, and more limpid; this was the only way he had of transmitting to her something that resembled joy. They exchanged their private signals. Once shut, the stable nullified words, as if they had never come to divide man from the other creatures that shared the earth with him; and thus even words like madness and scandal ceased to have meaning, replaced by an arcane perception like time.

"Listening to the dogs barking outside, to the woods shaken by the wind, the Duchess passed her hands over the horse's face, reading messages there that were always new and mysterious: 'What a crime,' she thought, 'that men work so frantically to take possession of logic. But I am not logic for him. No more is he logic for me. Therefore no one can do anything to hurt us.'

"When she put her arms around him, Alexandre tried to rear up, but he couldn't, because the Keeper had blocked his legs with the four gold rings which, after his death, went to a clandestine auction and then were conserved as blasphemous relics. The Duchess struggled vainly to open them, until her nails were broken; she gave up, on her knees, stroking his hooves, his shins scarred by brambles, kissing his bruises, feeling no disgust, and the horse responded by bending down his face toward her.

"Dominated by his powerful musculature, by the vision of his scrotum, dizzy with the odor from his coat, *Herself* endured the supremacy of natural forces over reason, and saw it as a mountain waiting to be conquered at the price of mortal danger.

"From their hiding places, the Superintendent of Menageries and the Keeper were listening so intensely to the silence around the stable that after a long time they thought they heard, perhaps because of autosuggestion, a woman's lacerating cry, a whinnying that went from soft to furious; in their ears the bestial entanglement came to embrace the night with the power of a hurricane where that which took on form and sound might simply have been the tension of their own conjectures.

"The two of them did not move a millimeter, they kept watching the lantern which, moving in the air, sent out intermittent flashes, hypnotizing them like a signal fire, unloosing visions: and then the window was transformed into a curtain that rose on a scene where the Duchess moved her sorceress' hands, and the animal's great member seemed drenched in blood, and the outpouring of semen seemed to go on forever.

"As soon as the Duchess came out of the stable, her face once more composed itself into regal dignity, smiling into the darkness: calm as a tigress after a good meal, they thought. The Keeper hastened to kiss her hand; he was certain, utterly certain, that it was dripping and bloody. And this certainty, which came from himself alone, sent him stamping into the stable like a general onto some deserted battlefield; he unfastened the rings, and down among the legs that were finally at liberty, he frenziedly erased with a rag that which perhaps didn't even exist, making the brick floor shine like a mirror."

This, perhaps, was the reality. Or perhaps . . .

What if the real story is told instead by those who insist that Maria Louisa of Hapsburg went into the Menagerie and closed herself up with Alexandre only to defy the gossip born out of the hearts of her enemies? Only to stroke the mane of a horse who had never betrayed her, never tried to saddle her, and who had raced with her in soaring happiness through the woods?

For a caress. . . .

EROS CAN BE A CARESS, A LETTER . . .

A cruel letter, about a caress, to a lover who has had many lovers:

" . . . I felt you in my fingertips, a woman no longer alone, no longer lost in the world of vain and selfish men you used to enjoy, a little bit lost, or maybe similar to them; I felt, touching you, the erotic complicity you have been searching for in so many other beds. In the fingers that outlined your profile, there was also emotion for the incomparable hour we were spending together, in an afternoon among the ones to be remembered for the beauty of nothing happening save for imperceptible things, like my caress.

Eros can be this, too: a trifle. My caress, which seemed to me full of the light of the returning summer, passed over you like the profoundest of souls, while you stared out the windows at the Lombardy poplars, and then you combed your hair, worried, with who knows what thoughts inside your silence.

My caress may have seemed like many others, but it had the light of an original gesture, a new amorous discovery, the kind we invent together like a delightful game. Just think, I was stroking you with a feeling of eternity.

Behind us there was the unmade bed, your pillow still veiled with your sweat, so good, my love . . . It wasn't just a question of love, but of ourselves being the complicated expedient that resolved itself into the caress, like the little cloud around the sun, up there, and the swallows shrilling, flying low.

Such a clear afternoon, looking toward the mountains, trembling at the thought of God. And this thought, too, passed through my caress.

It stayed there in our need to confide in each other, and to tell our worst secrets, just as the word desired to the point of madness cloys on the tongue of a mute. I measured my need for you in this caress. It was like when my cat Gina curls up on me with all her yearning to be the very beating of my heart that melts into her own.

I would have liked to lie down serenely beside you, in the shadow of the poplars aligned along the gravel bank, not to feel this regret, and these obscure hypotheses, about the many men who had you before I did. There was a little silence of the universe, did you notice?, in my fingertips.

How far away death was at that moment . . . In my gesture, I listened to your purity, which has survived in spite of everything, like the music of words which is there before the words are spoken. My caress made us perfect together. And you had the certainty that the way you had lived before, certain slightly base habits of yours, were dissolving forever while my fingers went down from your eyes to your throat, like the hand of a child who hardly touches the keyboard of a piano he doesn't know how to coax sounds from, with only the memory of a melody overheard, sublime."

"A caress that marvelled at its own unexpected enchantment.

The hand that is writing you this letter is the same one that caressed you the other day. In a little while it will lay down the pen. It will stay still, on the table.

I was thinking, caressing you: one day we'll be far away, we'll be a sudden shared thought, the kind that squeezes us in the vice of regret when we're walking down the street some bright morning; we'll be each other's buried memory.

It was a caress of farewell.

You didn't understand, you couldn't understand.

I gave you of myself all that it was possible for me to give, so that you can feel, in the future, only gratitude, when you want to, if you want to feel that.

What to tell you? Don't start throwing yourself away again, with one man, then another, just so they can vent their weak and distracted libidos for a moment.

I still have your warmth in my hand.

I feel a desire that's cruel to myself, self-destructive. I have to tell you: betray me right now, quickly, and do it so that I hear about it. In that way my longing for you will be less devouring.

I will always remember you. And passing beneath the windows of your house, I will always feel great sorrow whenever I look up. . . ."

The women who have loved me and whom I have let go. . . . There is a moment when everyone feels regret become remorse.

A loneliness makes my heart beat harder when, sometimes, I come back to places where, in certain periods I have been happy, and understood, looked after. In restaurants, at parties, in public places, I may happen to meet them with their new companions. In those moments, inside me, Eros would like to turn back into the child god with blindfolded eyes.

Often we even avoid speaking.

I look at these women, in contact with these men who seem to me obtuse, deprived of Eros' playful and knowing intelligence that I and my lost loves transmitted to one another, and which was the reason for their lives and love. I tell myself: "And to think that they loved me *with their fingernails*, as one of them kept telling me over and over."

I look again at the men who have replaced me. A sense of emptiness takes hold of me, and I tell myself: when they're in bed they're going to enjoy the amorous inventions *I* created with these women, loving them through hundreds of afternoons and nights dedicated to translating fantasy into reality. They make me feel that I've been robbed: they have taken over, and are delighting in, something that belongs to me and is mine, sacred, the art of my understanding of Eros, of how to inscribe it in a woman's intimacy just as I write a poem.

And so I see them as not only ignorant of a high art, blind and deaf to its graces, but nonetheless finding in their unworthy hands all the little treasures that I hid inside their present mistresses.

But it's my own fault, I let it happen.

Yesterday, going through writings I have kept, I read again a letter from a woman who was sensitive, although rather lost in looking for herself. She knew how to express herself well on the page. I gave her advice about that, too. Another relationship that I left behind. I question myself, I look for an answer. Perhaps because my senses are never satisfied: provoked perhaps by my avidity for my life not to be one and forever, but a thousand lives in one; perhaps by fear of death, through which I delude myself that other lives await me, more extraordinary than the one I've been living. . . .

And here is a passage from her letter:

"I've been thinking about you in these past weeks, and about those faint shadows of unknown origin that pass over a relationship and change its light and aspect. With no justification, inexplicably, the scene changes and our trifling or immense story falls apart, leaving us flung apart, strangers again. I know that I miss something and I'm sad. I know, too, that I've ended up in an empty place in your memory and that already your curiosity is moving you somewhere else; but what a shame to lose one another without regret or yearning, without even those words of affection that save people from diminishing, vanishing away. There's nothing left, everything is calm now, but there still remain bright images too hard for me to extinguish; in fact, at this very moment they're lighting up that shadowy room where, in the cigar smoke, your arms set free desires. . . ."

Big headlines in the newspaper: "ORAL SEX: IS IT RAPE?'No', Court Finds Husband Not Guilty; Sentence May Set Dangerous Precedent."

Oral sex is erroneously considered a banal act, a preamble. On the contrary, of all sexual relations it is the one that most involves erotic conscience. Therefore, if it is imposed on a woman, it can represent a violent coercion even more humiliating than forced penetration. And consideration should be given to oral coitus practiced by men upon women, who often prefer it. Few are the men who do not feel revulsion for this act. And, in performing it, they are generally awkward, hasty, completely unaware of the secret solicitations that nourish feminine nature.

J. S. was a fine actress: a few years of fame, a career ended by drug addiction. She cut herself off from drugs, but producers did not then cut off their cutting off of her. She was among the woman friends I was really fond of, to whom I listened with benevolent patience when she lectured me about what she defined as her nymphomania, telling me about the calvary of her obsessive complications.

J. S. used to glorify the special qualities of oral practices upon the female genitalia, expressing only scorn for her lovers' coarseness and hesitation. Their diffidence toward the *cunnilinctus* of antique memory was something she considered as an obscure, castrating denial by the male: a refusal to let face and breath dive into a woman's sex, into the maternal waters, the suffocating sea of life's first stirring. She would speak of the unconscious terror evoked by that marine odor, by that narrow opening like a shell's, by the hint of an abyss capable of subaqueous vampirism, all of which made them at last aware that they were still and forever traumatized children.

J. S. exaggerated, but there was truth in what she said.

Later the whiteness of the snow which loomed from the windows, or the street lights' coming on, would outline J. S.'s body with a troubling halo, as if she were being blotted out by figures lost in time. She slid downwards along my body; the half-moons of her breasts, the dark teardrops of her nipples, disappeared between my legs. Her forehead, her eyelids inclined, as if over a dish that was hers alone. I wanted to turn on the light, to break that arcane ritual with a quick flash, to lay the ghosts that swarmed from her head moving at the base of my belly, intent on that over which she reigned. I saw her as the head of an idol which took violent possession of its victims.

And then I remembered the Ilardi girl, Nuvola, the first one to teach me oral coitus when I was a little boy.

It happened one day when I had a fever.

Nuvola told me, as if she were telling me a fairy tale, that fevers need to be consoled, just like sadness, and she knelt between my legs, almost as if she wanted to pray to me, to worship me. She passed her fingers lightly over my shoulders, my breast, telling me that, if a boy didn't know about certain things, his brain might fill up with spiders and sick dreams, thoughts that skitter sideways like crayfish, and he might go crazy.

Finally she bent over me, kissing me first, all over my stomach, brushing her lips across my pubis where the first soft hairs were starting. She was singing very softly: a song, she told me, smiling, from the Venetian Po, from the time when the boatmen, proud as Turkish captains, would come back from their long voyages and be consoled by their wives. Then there was silence, the song died in her throat, and it was my sex that made it die there.

I listened to her breathing. And her mouth, as it moved, had the lightness of her breath. She took one of my hands and placed it on her head. An intense heat came from under her soft hair, while I could feel myself growing, inside her mouth, my entire self, including all my thoughts and dreams. It was the first time that I read my body sexually: I mean the marks, the special punctuation, the mysterious and invisible writings that we don't know we carry with us but which someone has inscribed on us; I discovered these and read them along with Nuvola, sharing her own surprise.

❧

I thought about the plants and flowers that suddenly, on a certain day in a season, grow and open because they are enfolded in springtime and they adorn themselves with the buds that spiral down from the sky the better for them to bloom. Nuvola was my springtime. And I, what flower, what plant was I? Nuvola didn't come back the next day or the next. I wandered around, looking for her, with the body's memory that an amputee must feel for the leg he no longer has, with the paradoxical certainty that it's still attached to him. It was really as if my sex had been amputated by Nuvola's mouth. And then I saw her one afternoon, her ballerina's legs under a short skirt, legs simultaneously so indecent and so pure, expressing the concept of liberty as they moved.

She was singing a song from the Venetian Po region as she walked with a man whose arm was around her waist. They disappeared behind a hedge. I came close to them, my heart tight, I crept as deeply into the hedge as I could go without risking being seen. All I could see were the man's shoes as he lay on the grass. It was when Nuvola stopped singing her soft song that I wanted to weep.

Thanks to her, I learned this, too: that a woman, with whom one has shared oneself, may secretly bestow her most intimate favors upon another man, forgetting the first one, not knowing that he's there, and knows, and witnesses. I learned that nothing is more terrible than this knowing, imagining, hearing. It is a cruelty that can kill every purity of the mind, every innocence of the heart.

The house in Piazza Inzani where I was born, in Parma, was a birdcage of twittering aunts. My grandmother Amelia had fifteen children: of the five males, one was dead, two were under arrest for political reasons, and another two, sought as subversives, had secretly slipped out of the country.

Some mornings, the ten aunts would come out together onto the terrace, where they called to each other, answering; in an airy agitation of multicolored negligees, a fluttering of hands that made me think of preening doves. I used to explore the aviary, slipping furtively into each of their rooms. I could go into Aunt Maria's, who spent her time at a little table, interrogating old Bolognese Tarot cards. Or into Aunt Giulia's, who kept trying to modify unpropitious destiny by constant prayer.

If, as I walked along the corridor, I put my ear against her door, I could hear her quiet orisons. It seemed to me that they never ceased.

Aunt Adele's room was the most inviting, with bentwood chairs, two tufted divans, a big brass bed. There Aunt Adele applied many kinds of face cream and continually tried on dresses. She was a mixture of fine and coarse: green eyes, but heavily outlined; aristocratic cheekbones, but a boldly painted mouth; robust arms, delicate hands; thick legs, tiny feet. The sisters constantly scolded her, which only made her provoke them more. She was a magnet for scandal. She wasted her earnings in buying junk jewelry, especially rings and bracelets; she wandered nude or half-dressed through the birdcage, wearing transparent kimonos, delighted if she managed to upset her sisters. She was pleased to be considered a shameless flirt, and boasted that she couldn't count all the men she'd had: of every one of them, however, she had kept something — photographs, even the most trivial objects — and her lovers' souvenirs now filled an armoire. The junkyard queen of love, she laughed. When it was time for her to depart for a happy land far away, she would manage to bring the armoire, too.

I would run into unknown men who left their motorbikes in the courtyard. Before they closed the door of Aunt Adele's room behind them, they would give me a distracted pat.

But the room that attracted me most deeply was my Aunt Carmen's. Unlike her sister Adele, she despised her own corporeal beauty, which had been manifested in an all but absolute perfection: her Spanish features, inherited from the paternal side, took on mystery within the oval of her Emilian face, a magic circle surrounding the vibrant and proud physiognomy; and from this contrast came a kind of languid tenderness, a sensuality of great spiritual depth. She made me think of the markings that Nature traces, mysteriously, capriciously, upon a human being just as on a plant or a flower.

Trying to understand her own allure, searching in the mirror so intently that it became an obsession, Aunt Carmen fell into a conflicted psychological state from which she could see no exit. At some moments she felt only self-contempt; at others, haughtiness and pride. And if the self-contempt made her feel unworthy of so much natural beauty, the pride impeded her from ever sharing it. What man was good enough to rise to her own charms for even the most ephemeral affair, not even to mention a display of more enduring passions which she imagined to be in any case vulgar? All this caused her great anguish, which, in addition to tormenting Carmen, was mirrored by the disorder of her room, where she finally concluded that physical beauty was a kind of crime that destroys peace of mind and transforms one into a creature excluded from the world.

Unlike Aunt Adele, therefore, she was waiting for the passing years to make her old, with the hope of one day reading the marks of ruin in her face: only as an old woman would she be free to dispose of herself. And the men who came at night to be with Aunt Adele sometimes might see Carmen unmoving at the end of the corridor, seeming to wait for them in the shadows, but if they took even one step toward her, she was already gone . . .

I asked myself, amazed, how it was that Aunt Carmen kept on papering her walls with pictures of famous actors and actresses: Rudolf Valentino, Greta Garbo, Marlene Dietrich . . . Didn't this apparent worship contradict her refusal to idolize the body? I understood later, when I discovered among the jumbled objects piled in her room an authentic collection of *oddities*: biographies, diaries, true confessions, rare editions, too.

For the first time I found myself reading pages that were inspired by sexual ambiguity.

I was struck, in particular, by the secret diary of Rudolf Valentino, the "dark god adored by millions of women." Some ponderous wit nicknamed him *Pink Powder-Puff*, and the *Chicago Tribune* wrote as follows: "It would have been much better if this fluffy pink thing, who never makes a move without his makeup, this handsome son of a gardener, Mister Guglielmi, alias Valentino, had been drowned in a pond before being imported into the United States." Valentino married two noted lesbians: the first, Jean Acker; the second, more restless, was Natasha Rambova.

In this secret and in some ways terrible diary of the actor who has retained his place in popular history as the symbol *par excellence* of the male seducer of women, Aunt Carmen underlined two passages:

"*June 27.* I can't stand it any longer. Tomorrow I board the ship. When I think that Natasha is in Paris, in that woman's arms . . . What an atrocious thing jealousy is!"

"*July 5.* The Paris night has separated us even more.

"She refused me again . . . At four in the morning I slipped out of the hotel. Outside, I wandered the streets of this fascinating

romantic city, not knowing where I could go, just to breathe again
. . . It's as though I'm being devoured by flames, I'm burning with
desire to make love, and Natasha won't have me! A beautiful boy
followed me for a quarter of an hour, and finally he spoke to me
outside the Opéra . . . I went back to his place, and when we started
up the stairs he was already all over me, kissing me. It was as if I'd
been unchained . . . We made love like two tigers until dawn."

And in Aunt Carmen's room I also read the confessions of
Mercedes De Acosta, poetess and Hollywood screenwriter in the
thirties and forties. Mercedes, the great seductress of famous
women, of divas above suspicion, stars considered unattainable.

Greta Garbo was crazy about her. Their love, consummated in a
lodge in the Sierra Nevada, ended when Mercedes told all in her
autobiography: "Days of absolute perfection and harmony with the
nature that surrounded us." There are photographs that testify to
these days: images of the two women naked beside a lake. Isadora
Duncan wrote an erotic poem for Mercedes De Acosta: "My kisses
are like golden bees — darting down — between your knees . . . "
Marlene Dietrich courted Mercedes with great masses of tulips,
and when she sent them back, complaining that their shape was
overly phallic, Marlene sought pardon by sending pink roses twice
a day, always with the same message: "Our love will be eternal." De
Acosta boasted, "I can take any woman away from any man."
Teased by Truman Capote, she snapped, "Ask my husband. I even
brought a girlfriend on our honeymoon." Mercedes always kept a
note from Dietrich, in which the Blue Angel confided her own
creed: "I make love with anyone I like. I don't care if it's a man or a
woman."

Female bisexuality, when manifested in relations with another woman, is often seen as an unambiguous homosexual deviation, stemming from perversion.

In the majority of cases, this is not a pathological entity but a plant that grows from a shoot of autoeroticism. Whoever emphasizes the importance of narcissism is right: a woman, especially in adolescence or in early youth, may seek out her own sexuality through that of a friend. It is erotic potential that is searching for a form; the discovery, in a similar body, of certain capacities which the subject herself cannot yet consciously dominate; the igniting of a "limpid viciousness" which is no paradox, and which exists as an uneasy expression of curiosity.

I read, "Apart from the indeterminacy of the factors of masculinity and femininity — whichever sex one may belong to, every individual possesses in varying proportions both factors — we must recognize that women are more frequently bisexual than men."

There is a passage by Roberto Longhi — in *Correggio and the Chamber of St. Paul* — whose insights adapt perfectly to this discourse, even if they may appear extraneous. Longhi says that Michelangelo might well have exclaimed, as Picasso wickedly did of Braque: *Correggio c'est ma femme!*

Within the sensibility of every woman is the dream of Eros, painted inside her mind by a master's hand. A Michelangelo is there, a Correggio is there. To use Longhi's words, "there exists the faculty of liberating one's own introverted temperament, of subjectifying one's profound inclination toward the sexual aspect, a succubic yielding before Michelangelo's virile aggressiveness . . . That rampant energy, that 'convex tumidity,' blend into the deeply subtle delineations and 'concave' graces of Correggio."

I've listened to so many confessions from women, and from women they loved, too. What moved them was not so much the ambiguity of their passion but their passion for ambiguity. By which I mean that they were serene about certain experiences, capable of controlling them as occasional acts, illuminated by a sense of play throughout the course of their own psychological equilibrium. The first awareness of sexual reciprocity — at a time when they feared masculine aggressiveness and the black myth of rape — came through those caresses, those kisses . . .

My friend A. B. confesses to me:

"Yes, it's happened that I identify myself with women, in a mutual yearning for impossible love, since with men I was disappointed and disappointing. Eros as mutual consolation, Eros as friendship, too: a female friendship which a man couldn't understand. . . ."

I ask her about her first time.

"I was sixteen. It happened at night. My girl friend and I were sleeping in the same bed with her mother. We began to stroke each other, to kiss, excited, too, because we were afraid her mother would wake up. At first we did it with pleasure, the beauty of feeling our hearts in our throats, then with a kind of stealthy joy, the happiness of living through something secret, forbidden, right next to a severe grownup who was sleeping turned on her side . . . Other times, too, with other women. I especially liked insinuating myself on top of them, as if I were doing what a man does . . . The excitement always began in vexation or melancholy, because there wasn't any man around who was worthy of having our sensibility and sexuality . . . or because of the dissatisfaction men gave us, wretched lovers who didn't know what to do with their members or with their souls."

I have memories of certain amorous games.

When two women would begin to express themselves, in front of me, no longer needing words, using the silent communication of their touch. Against the brightness of the window, one friend was leaning her head against the other's shoulder, holding her close in the arc of her arm. The vision of their nude backs, close together, while outside the windows the wind pulled down the leaves in little spirals, evoked the figures on oriental temples. And the scene of two women undressing, watching one another from opposite sides of the bed, exerts a sacred attraction, too: even in the most impure circumstances, this prelude still conserves its purity. The one scrutinizes herself in the other with a nostalgia for herself which surfaces little by little, as she strips her body bare, and the more ambiguous and unhealthy the situation, the stronger grows the nostalgia for an intimacy which once, long ago, was uncontaminated.

IRONIES, IRONIES . . .

I

In the Portico d'Ottavia, men from the Roman underworld are playing pallamuro. In these unthinkable subterranean spaces which the same men use as a shooting gallery, bullet holes multiply almost as you look at them. Two murdered bodies were found there recently.

Here vastness reigns, reds and blacks that seem to have been painted by the hand of Scipio; the acrid odor of Tiber water seeps in, stagnating under windows and peepholes, between glimpses of distant bridges. I used to go there often. Some encounters are possible only there. If I continue living in Rome, it's because the city has also this perverse power: it generates, and quickly degenerates, astonishing crossroads of existence.

That's how it was with Donata.

I must point out that *pallamuro* differs from both handball and *pelote*. It's a game without any past and certainly without a future. Perhaps it exists only at Portico d'Ottavia. The player flings the ball with a huge leather glove, like a black fin; the target, activated mechanically, moves rapidly. You have to hit the three red spots. It is a metaphor of the struggle against time. The balls describe senseless trajectories, accompanied by shrieked curses; the man's hand receives the ball's violent blow and throws it back obtusely, exactly, just a little further. Isn't time itself violence, an end in itself, going and coming back?

Donata — I learned this very quickly — was a violent egotist, dual in nature: part ball, part mitt. Fierce and useless like the men who play *pallamuro*.

She was sprawled in the iron chair next to mine at the edge of the underground room: the balls whistled past us like the nighttime bullets that found the Roman gangsters' designated victims. You could sense in her a sexuality no less dark and menacing than this place: eighteen years old at most, a female odor like the Tiber, great hypermammalian breasts. I asked myself what she could possibly be doing here. What were her relations with the players, probably murderers, draped in leather aprons that gleamed with the sweat that flooded their bare arms and shoulders; and the other ones, leaning against the wall, who called out their bets in raucous shouts?

Some stirring of genital excitement led Donata to a gesture that seemed casual but which was entirely obscene. The fingers of her right hand, with their red-lacquered nails, slid along the inside of her jeans-clad thigh and began to give quick squeezes to her pubis. I turned to stare at her. She didn't stop. Nor did she worry about the rebounding balls that could smash her skull. Finally she smiled at me. Cannibal teeth, I thought.

We didn't move until the players stopped. No one was left down here in the dim underground space. Now it looked like a marketplace after the market has ended: a few rare lights still lit; the butchers' aprons on hooks, the fin-like leather gloves hanging from a rack, still shaped into the furious clutch of the hands that had worn them. Balls scattered on the ground. A huge letter *A* on the wall across from us and nightbirds at the windows.

"Let's go to my place," she said.

The only thing Donata communicated to me was emptiness. Her body moved with the jerky disharmony of carnal sordidness. So what drew me, then, along behind her as she walked briskly through the dark, showing how well she knew the city's meanderings? Disgust? Her all too obvious intent of profiting from my presumed naïveté?

Something more and something less. I was stimulated by her nullity. Not in any metaphysical sense, but in very fact that nullest of nullities that insinuates itself among the little beauties and cruelties of life, providing in its way a connection between them. Donata was enticing me with a lack of attraction so perfect as to be irresistible.

In that sense, it was a gratifying night.

One room. An unmade bed against the wall, with a fake leopard-skin cover. African war drums atop the headboard. A Somali spear. On the floor, dusty stacks of newspaper. I pretended not to see the headlines about various crimes. Then shoes, everywhere, mostly men's; the tips, of every color, protruded like clowns' noses. But those who habitually prowled this room, presumably the same ones who played *pallamuro*, had disseminated other relics here and there: briefs, undershirts, belts. The bathroom door was open and an azure lightbulb lit the loneliness. The window, which let in very little air, was at sidewalk level (we were in the basement of a building in San Giovanni).

Donata turned off the light. She carefully pulled the curtain across the window. I asked her why she was doing that.

"So they don't know I'm here," she answered. "So they don't know I exist."

"But who?"

"Men," she said brusquely.

"What men?"

Impassive look.

"There are all kinds," I suggested. "Intellectuals, for example, or cops. Which ones are you afraid of? The *pallamuro* guys?"

"Men. All of them. I'd like to see them all hung up by the feet in Piazzale Loreto." She didn't say anything else.

I would have liked to point out to her that I too belonged to the race she scorned. But it would have been an error. It was clear that, while she fled from male reality, she was seduced by male nothingness, to the same degree that female nothingness had attracted me that night. That's what I was in her eyes. We were two nothings that drew one another like magnets.

I drank Donata's aphrodisiac nullity to the dregs. I sought it throughout her anatomy, as through the secret turnings of a labyrinth. I followed all the disentanglings of her hair, waist-length, raven, dirty. The newborn babe sucks nourishment from the mother's nipple for its still-fetal nothingness; I used this girl's huge breasts. I explored her belly, her weedy pubis, imprinted on her like the menacing letter *A* on the wall of the *pallamuro* court.

For her part, Donata explored me, groping with all the blindness of her spirit: and everyone knows the blind are masters of the dark.

Several times I feared that I would dissolve into that belly. I comprehended the wisdom of antique texts: the Talmud, Zohar, Isaiah. Donata incarnated the triad of Chaldeo-Assyrian demonology (the most exact, in my opinion): Lilù, the incubus-demon; Lilitu, the succubus-demon; and Ardat Lili, the servant of the first two, who chooses the lovers to be devoured by them: the phallus, of course, and all the other Adamic material that composes them. Many bright metallic things flashed through my mind. But one of them, silvery, in the shape of a pointed heart, stood out among the rest; it wasn't a mirage but a real blade: the Somali spear!

I could use that if I had to.

When I opened the slit of window, the first sunlight glowed on Donata, panting and sweaty. Like me.

All she did was cross her legs and smile at me. The detached smile of someone who expects a return for her hospitality.

"What's your house like?" she asked.

"Big," I answered, looking around the suffocating room. "There's a view."

"Do you live with anybody?"

"I used to live with my wife. Now I don't live with anybody, no."

"Let's go," she said.

I had invaded even the nullity of her environment. She was determined to invade mine.

She didn't give me time to object. She came out with a single bag and her war drums in a net sling. And so, I thought, nothingness doesn't care about the past or the future, it only needs itself and its devouring music. We got into the car. Immediately she had me make several detours through the byways of San Giovanni, sordid stretches between imposing houses.

"Stop here!" she ordered.

She told me to wait for her. She reappeared from a doorway, balancing a birdcage where little birds of various species teetered. From two other houses — doubtless those of intimate friends — she emerged with big plastic bags full of clothes, and the friends in person, wearing the faces of the *pallamuro*-playing assassins, helped load dresses, cartons, record-players, rolled-up posters. Not, obviously, ever deigning to greet me by even a nod.

And so, Donata was being reborn from the ashes. Her perfidious calculations about me were being transmuted into the fullness of joy. We continued to pause here and there, she would keep making me stop by shouting a sudden command. She indicated doors, windows. She would come running back down to the car, animals under her arms; dogs and cats now joined the birds, things on top of things, revealing an existential backstage area in Donata that I could never have imagined, and that kept being translated with endless flourishes into an object, an animal, a mysterious box, a little package.

Other men with unkempt beards, bruised girls, mothers who were obviously pimping for their daughters, porters with corruption painted on their faces, came stepping right behind Donata, each bearing a contribution. The car was overflowing. I could imagine my apartment; with the difference that while I had invaded Donata's refuge, savoring the taste of obliteration, her taking possession of mine prefigured, beyond permanent settlement, the triumph of superconsumerism.

"One moment, my dear," I told her.

I stopped the car under the obelisk in Piazza del Popolo.

"Just a minute."

I left her there boldly smoking, her elbow out the window. There she was, with the satisfied ferocity of a lion tamer, among birds who were singing their own green color, dogs pawing at the rear window, boxes tumbling into other boxes, dresses blowing in the wind. The car was like a little circus, already being surrounded by suspicious cops.

I went into the Caffé Canova and came out again immediately, hiding behind a stranger. In certain circumstances, it's really lovely to be vile. I fled toward the Pincio. I hadn't run with this exhilaration in years; and I was surprised that I could not only reach a respectable speed but feign such nonchalance.

I never knew what happened to Donata, or to my car (I did report it to the police as stolen). I never went back to Portico d'Ottavia to watch the gangsters play *pallamuro*. I read in the newspaper that another dead body was found in an underground passage there. Could it be Donata? The victim had long red-lacquered nails. Nullity tends toward nullity and — in this case — becomes metaphysical, eternal. There is, finally, a justice for everything.

II

The windows of Sybille Weiser's house look out over the Isola Tiberina. In a living room that looks like an artist's studio, lamps make Viennese enamels by Mohn glow even more, wash over huge enlargements of Egon Schiele's models, and light up objects by the artists of Gabbonz. Among all Rome's powers, there is also this: of creating oases that enclose the styles and tastes of other peoples.

This house is my favorite nighttime refuge. And since Sybille is a mistress of stratagems, I privately call her "the lady of a thousand and one nights." She continues to welcome me, gladly, at whatever hour. She esteems me. In her own way, she loves me. But we decided to maintain ourselves in a state of *before*, where — my friend is categorical about this — it's amusing to invent preambles which are, perhaps, the best part of a relationship.

"Isn't dawn the most evocative part of the day?" she suggests. "And thirst, just before you drink at a cool spring in the mountains, isn't such a torturing pleasure — something priceless?"

Sometimes she almost convinces me. About *before* — before things happen, they are more beautiful. I agree, joking: life, before death happens, is surely more beautiful than death itself? You have to keep up with things.

Sybille is thirty. Her body reminds of the woman who, in Klimt's *Golden Fish*, flaunts her inviting buttocks at the viewer. When it happens that we're waiting for the dawn, alone, and then she goes to bed, undressing casually in front of me, I am exhorted to consider that Klimt's intentions should have led him to entitle that painting "Before."

"Do you see how brilliant *before* is? Desire is at its peak, you feel irresistibly drawn to lift your hand, to just barely touch me . . . But the only thing you're touching is the illusion of a painting." She urges me: "Go ahead, touch me."

I obey. But I can't quite make myself believe that her buttocks are the fruit of illusion. I confess this to her. She replies:

"That's because you don't know how to detach yourself from your past." She falls into a play on words: "You never made love to the *before* before you met me?"

"Never," I admit.

"That's a vice you need to get over. You're such a stubborn consumer of *afterwards*, you're just like a chain smoker. You have to begin. The important thing is to throw away the very first cigarette that you automatically stick in your mouth . . . Go on, try it."

She tells me what to do:

"You get undressed too. Get in bed with me. We'll sleep together, that's all. We'll just feel the warmth of each other's bodies, and in our mutual warmth there's already coitus, already orgasm. Close your eyes, relax, you'll see I'm right."

I do close my eyes. I keep my hand, barely in reach of her thigh, immobilized. She starts telling me about longings it would be easy to satisfy, but that beauty resides in their not being satisfied . . .

"Are you relaxing? Are you sleepy?"

"No, Sybille. I'm sorry. But don't worry, you go to sleep. Leave the *before* to me, I'll watch over it . . . Before creation. When there was no trouble, or loneliness, or impossible temptations . . . "

"Wasn't I right?"

"Right, yes. And then came the fiat lux. . . . Go to sleep, Sybille. It'll be dawn soon anyway. The light will be . . . light. And I can get up and go away, leaving you embracing our *before*, who's such a fantastic lover."

Sybille, of course, loves Schönberg. She urges me again:

"Go back to being a child. And, just as you used to count sheep, think very hard about *Pierrot lunaire*. Ah, the "Red Mass" Lied, where Pierrot climbs up on the altar and shows the faithful the Host all red with blood. It's his heart! He's clutching it in his fingers and he offers it as a warning to them, telling them not to dissipate themselves in the banalities of love, in the fire of reality that turns everything to ash so quickly."

I try. Now I hate Pierrot as much as Schönberg: "I can't help it, Sybille, I love Verdi and Rossini."

"Hack work."

I overreact, I touch her. But in the name of an ideal of poetry, of melodies that no one has ever managed to extinguish in my heart. Sensuality has nothing to do with it. The *before* remains intact:

"Too many tears," she says scornfully, turning on her side in the *Golden Fish* position. And I do the same, achieving the more banal position of someone who simply turns his back. "Always too much passion," she adds.

. . . but on this night the tears and overabundance of passion are Sybille's own. I gather that one of her lovers — with whom, unlike me, she had never shared a *before* — had left her with no warning, treating her brutally.

It's to me alone that Sybille concedes the rare privilege of the *before*, of which she considers others unworthy. And there are a lot of them, she cries, all destined for her scorn.

I should consider myself fortunate. It's not every day that one finds oneself the favorite of a fascinating woman. One who knows Schönberg's atonal "countersense" by heart.

III

This episode happened between finding myself, still a child and in innocence, next to Albina Savi's nudity against the stones in the dry riverbed, and my first time with Ada Vitali, at Ghiare, the village of scythes.

I saw curiosity about women grow in the men around me. I made two discoveries at once: I discovered that discovering their curiosity made me happy. I was a young boy who wandered alone through the outlying neighborhoods of Parma. I would stop in front of the cottage where Fabrizia Orlandini lived, she who was known as "The Unmasked Ball."

The house looked dejected, standing directly across from an unfinished building whose construction had gone on for years: conceived as a school, it had undergone continual and rather mysterious interruptions. There it stayed, with its five floors traced over emptiness, without walls, like a great cement scaffold, with the anonymous arrogance that unfinished buildings have. Nothing else in that whole zone of the periphery. The cottage, a witty subject; the building, a dotty king.

I used to hide and look at the unsteady beams, the reed fencing, the king's battered crown. A young boy is a highly skilled detective. Since he need not resolve the enigma of life, he searches out and often solves phenomena erroneously considered marginal. And so I noticed the pantomime that men kept organizing with a single purpose: to see inside Fabrizia's windows. Later I too came to know her as the most daring and seductive exhibitionist in our city.

"They're going to look at God's own body in the Orlandini girl," shouted an individual who was climbing up the building. "They're taking their places for the Unmasked Ball."

The climbers were of several types. Stonemasons who were not stonemasons; geometers and building inspectors who were definitely unqualified. Before venturing aloft, they would take off their jackets and vests, put on workmen's caps made out of folded newspaper, and roll up their shirtsleeves. They were really lawyers, doctors, teachers, transformed for the occasion into clumsy acrobats. Having conquered an observation post, they would wander helpfully about, carrying a few bricks as if they couldn't decide where to put them, never losing sight of the window down below.

Fake verifiers of land records and self-appointed municipal inspectors, wearing fur-collared overcoats, also made it to the top. With firm steps on the shaky catwalk they would give orders in a loud firm voice to sub-officials who weren't visible, simply because they didn't exist. And it wasn't difficult to deduce, even from my hiding-place, that only stray cats and a few doubtful mice and, most numerous of all, a clump of dusty reeds were listening to their tirades about abuses in the construction trades in Parma.

Next the poets climbed up.

They pretended to be gathering flowers which had never bloomed, there among the weeds that clung to the scaffolding. Creeping along the balcony and looking down toward Fabrizia's window, they rocked back and forth between the felicity of their senses and a vocation, not unusual in lyric temperaments, for cosmic suicide, or rather the risk of falling all the way down. I saw one of them who really did bring a bunch of roses with him; for as long as he kept looking, he held it showily against his shoulder. When he left, he threw it into the reeds and the wind tore it apart and scattered petals on the air.

And finally the honest ones went up. I mean the ones who felt no need of disguising themselves with paper hats and rolls of blank blueprints in order to spy on the cottage. They improvised no dialogues with cats and birds, but yielded to the seduction of ocular profanation with eagerness and candor, staring down frankly into the house with the stance and attitude of some staunch watcher of the seas.

The pantomime was lively, misunderstandings were frequent. Emerging onto the terrace, the phony stonemason might encounter someone prowling along the brink with a bouquet of roses clutched in his hand, or feigned building inspectors trying to convince a chimney swift that the march of events, such as this building's perpetual state of incompletion, was difficult both to explain and to correct. But delight in their common transgression and the recognition of how alike they all were created a virile complicity that cancelled any embarrassment. Thus two or more gentlemen would be peering down together, exchanging smiles and lighting each other's cigarettes.

. . . there was a particular window in the cottage. The curtains were imprudently held back with heavy red silk cords; objects were visible inside: an indiscreet penumbra surrounded them, out of which the music of a record on the gramophone rose up. A little dog in an armchair displayed admirable modesty. The things in the room seemed poised to pay homage to the figure everyone was awaiting. And then there she was, in all her harmonious beauty; but now Fabrizia was pretending to talk to her little dog, or glancing toward the corridor, chattering expansively to mysterious presences (nonexistent servants and family members), not trying to see them, but to be seen. And to be seen at her best, she flung herself into improvisations which proved that she, too, was an actress on a paradoxical stage. Who, in reality, was the subject of the pantomime: the woman or the men who watched her?

The Orlandini girl's nudity kept moving within the window, from light into shadow, changing its shape with every reflection, every false perspective. Now her body appeared tall and regal; now, shorter and with larger breasts. She chatted animatedly with her resident phantoms just as her watchers did with theirs, or she laughed at jokes no one had told her. All that she did enhanced her graces.

Her mood would change, as if all around her were a crowd of presences, sometimes sad, sometimes happy, who caused her to alternate gestures of sadness and indolence with bursts of aggressive sensuality. She would bend down, pretending to pick something up from the floor, to show off her buttocks. She would simulate sudden fatigue, sinking onto the divan or into an armchair, one leg flung over the overstuffed arm, her pubis spotlighted. Her exhibitionism attained its diapason when she knelt down and put her ear next to her dog's nose, whereupon it barked obligingly, thus taking part in the performance: the perfect spirals of her back and thighs offered the watchers an irresistible vision of the baroque. Fabrizia disappeared, and the idea of not seeing her again caused hearts to feel despair. But suddenly, happiness returned, because the mirror, as if by enchantment, was now reflecting her inside its frame while she with her tapering fingers applied her lipstick. She had planned even these little touches, that was clear. One understood this from all the time she took, as if her lips were a vast surface. Caught in that pose, standing lightly on tiptoes, her pelvis tilted back, she deserved applause.

And while Fabrizia Orlandini showed off her charms, the watchers, perched on top of the unfinished building with their eyes fixed on the window, automatically uttered remarks which were meant to justify their presence, but only made it pathetic:

"They're never going to finish this school, it's a scandal!" affirmed a prince of the courtroom whose sleeves were rolled up.

"Yes, in fact, I came up here to verify what damage there is," replied a reporter for the local *Gazette*. "I'm going to have to write a very tough article."

"I'm thinking about our children, understand? They'll end up getting their learning, their culture, down by the river, or in the fields, or on the cathedral steps!"

"The government ought to intervene."

"Oh, we're intervening!" an assessor of public instruction assured them.

⁂

Someone speculated that the building would never go beyond its present stage for the simple reason that, were it to be completed, the body of Fabrizia Orlandini would no longer be open to exploration, with the unthinkable consequence that education (sexual rather than scholastic) would suffer.

A poet, aiming his rose at the window, scoffed: "The government is a band of thieves. Who else filled their pockets with the money to finish this school?"

The assessor rose up: "That's a know-nothing thing to say. Worse: it's fascist!"

But not even his leftist outburst drew anyone's gaze away from the cottage.

"Soon, very soon, dear friend, the Right is coming back to power!" announced a former member of Decima Mas, but the Memento Audere Sempre was quickly subdued, the other guy gave up trying to provoke the assessor, because now Fabrizia was preparing for her grand finale. And so the watcher forgot about cudgelling reds and passed into a dream: that of one day going into the Orlandini house, creaking his boots and wearing his scarf, to reduce the optical distance between himself and Fabrizia:

"We will return, my friend. Just as she will return." And at this point he lost all restraint. He pointed toward the window: "Let us look at her without cavils of pretense: she is part of us, she is a marvel, every one of us carries an Orlandini in his heart!"

Indeed, when Fabrizia caressed her body . . . her hand became that of an unseen man, invisible behind her chair, exploring her thighs with the most delicate lust (in the play of light and shadow it really seemed to be a hand that wasn't hers). What precise and perverse harmony! And when she stroked her breasts, her belly, her temples . . . The exhibition over, she looked up, toward the terrace of the half-built structure, with the smile of the protagonist who thanks the public at the end of the play. She made a bow and really did leave the room. The nostalgic watcher led the applause, saying:

"We will return because, unlike you, we've got the courage to impose, not reality on our eyes, but our eyes on reality. With virile boldness."

The wild applause floated up to the clouds.

The Orlandini house, the never-finished school, were, in their way, unchanging Italy.

THE JARGON OF EROS

When I started coming back to Parma, it sometimes happened that Maura Fiori would send girls to me, friends of hers, who were like messages in a bottle and through whom she managed to keep me closed up in a hotel room, happy to weave the strands of my life together. Sometimes she would leave me little notes in which, with affectionate sarcasm, she urged me to have a good time and stay calm, adding, "I've got so many things to tell you."

She did in fact tell them to me, through her friends; young women, all from old Parmigiano families, knowing the dialect and the slang, the ceremonies of the senses that are so absolutely our own.

In this way, Maura sought to restore to me the flavor of my city from which I had stayed away so long; just as she tried to keep me from rushing through the days of my visits, restraining my wish to leave again, and soothing me into a pleasant waiting for something unforeseen.

With these girls I was able to speak the language of my home again. I realized, as I spoke, that I had lost the use of a great part of the dialect, just as you lose dexterity if you stop practicing some skill. Words and ways of saying things that, for my amiable visitors, were playful coded schemes, but which for me were the very salt of life. It was this that attracted me, even more than their love-games, which also gave certain forgotten erotic rituals back to me. These came from a time in which peasant morality made rules that were all its own: as when, for example, the women threshing the wheat, in their brief rests behind the hedgerows, would relieve their male companions of their cumbersome sperm, not so much to offer them pleasure, but out of the conviction — as a country proverb says — that loaded testicles confuse the head and distract from work.

The dialect, the slang, began to surge up, simple and joyous. More than lovers, we were happy birds trilling to each other, preening on a branch. It was as if I were discovering a hieroglyphic language incised on rosy backs, firm buttocks, along the fine scissoring legs typical of Emilian women.

Then the girls left the room, and I opened the window, breathing the dawn air. Parma was splotched with snow. Against the snowy sky, the tip of the Duomo; a little moon, like the lighted angel up above.

*

I realized I no longer knew what day it was. And that the concert of the first sparrows, a blackbird's whistle, corresponded to the language with which Maura Fiori's friends and I had possessed one another: it still seemed to float in the air, like the persistent corporeal perfumes of the sprightly presences who had just left the room.

*

In Po, where I grew up, the male member changes its name according to the profession of its owner. Thus the carters of Arginotto affectionately call it *alberobello* (beautiful tree) or *pingherlone* (fatso, fatty); the boatmen of Barbamaco speak playfully of their *remo ghignante* (tricky oar) or their *prua*, (prow); the smugglers of Mirasole mysteriously prefer *Fratello Branca* (carabiniere, sharpshooter), or the *red seminarian*, or the *91 gun*.

All dialects, slang, and argot display extraordinary possibilities for wit.

The popular euphemism most widely used in Italy and the western Romance countries is obviously *figa*, fig, for the vulva. Fruits in general seem to lend themselves, either because of some iconic resemblance or deeper unconscious affinities, as metaphoric vehicles for the female sexual organ. In the northern regions, *brugna*, for plum; in various dialects of both north and south, *muljàga*, apricot, prevails.

The cat and mouse are often evoked in denominating the sexual organ. In Reggio Emilia, the vulva is both *sorgàvala* and *bùs del gàt*, mousetrap and cat-hole. Other zoological metaphors include *parpàja*, butterfly (especially near Norceto), *passaréna*, little sparrow, *pisàcra*, snipe — which may owe its use to a paraphonic echo of *pisciare*, (to piss). The typical *barbiza* (from *barbiz*, mustache) and the many variants of *pelosa* (hairy) are known all over Italy — *varpelosa* (hairy valley) and *La madre de le sante* (the mother of saints) are popular in Belli — again, particularly in the north.

The names of musical instruments often occur in erotic slang. The most common are worth mentioning: *chitàrra, chitarénna* (guitar), popular in Tuscany as well. Many terms, however, derive from personal names. *Bertagna* from Bertha (Germanic in origin), *Barnarda* (from the Veneto, Lombardy, and Reggio Emilia), obviously a form of Bernarda, *Flippa* (Filippa), especially in the Friuli and Veneto region; *Gnéza*, from Agnese.

The palatal phoneme "*gn*" occurs frequently in names for the vulva. This phoneme is charged with phonosymbolic values, linked to the idea of "lament" or "something simultaneously tender and disgusting": we find it in the Romanesco and Foggian *frégna, parpagnacca* from Tuscany, Emilia, and the Veneto, the Tuscan *fogna*, the slang *zampogna*, the Venetian *zgnéra*. And *gnocca*.

The typical *Siora Luigia*, Sister Gigi, recurs in Emilia as in many other regions; but *Luigione* (Big Louie) exists as well, to indicate the male organ. This name seems to be a favorite appellation, who can say why?

Once more in my part of the country, you might hear an old man grumble as a girl in a miniskirt passes by: "*La fa vèdr al nùmor dla cà*," which is to say, "She's showing you her house number."

The typical metaphors which allude to the male member mostly use the very image into which it is transformed in dreams, starting with the most common one, *uccello*, bird, a euphemism that modesty has made taboo now, causing it to lose its earlier innocent and fantastic meaning. In texts on folk sayings we read, "Also *caz, 'caso'* in the popular rhyme *naz bel caz*[1], *'naso bel caso'* (ah, Pinocchio!) is to be understood as an euphemism by means of the phonetic

---

1. 'great nose, great hose'

alteration of *cas, cazzo* [virile member], from which it is probable that *ciccio* [sausage] derives, especially in the Veneto."

Folk euphemisms for the member that are most strongly figurative and amusing are usually highly compressed descriptive phrases, such as the classic *cresinmàn,* for *crèssa in man,* "cresce in mano": "it grows in the hand"; or *carna ca se zlonga,* "carne che si allunga" = "stretchy meat." The often-heard *ghigno* may be set beside the Neapolitan *chigno,* "trickster."

In a text on sayings from the Val Padana I read: "The locution *s la ja mètta in fila la stafila la lòn'na,* 'se li mette in fila staffila la luna' (line them up end to end and they'll loop around the moon), said of a woman who is considered frivolous in her attachments, reveals a widespread use of the neutral pronoun. The demonstrative pronoun *chi lù,* 'this one,' indicative of the male member, is almost always accompanied by an eloquent gesture of the hand."

The range of terminology for sexual acts is equally vast.

I love the idea of a conversation — whispered on a summer's night, behind a wall, perfumed with linden flowers — between one of those young women called seagulls because they fly freely, and a man who prides himself on his command of the local slang.

She asks him, "What do you want to do with me?"

"*Un bacio ammobiliato,* a kiss with all the trimmings," replies the cunning linguist.

"And what do you want me to do?"

"*Polpastrelli a la truccante,*" her fingertips masturbating him with the delicacy a safecracker brings to the combination of a bank vault, known as the *truccante,* the bag of tricks.

"Then what?"

"Give me *un bicérino stélante*, a glassful of stars." Fellatio, envisioned as a glass of rare liquor, symbol of both container and its contents; executed so exquisitely by the woman that the man falls back, his ecstatic gaze turned upwards, scrutinizing the stars, thus becoming *stélante*, his head filled with sparkles from his own blood and from the firmament.

" . . . And let's finish in beauty with a *culofigato*."

A word, as I have said on other occasions, that is a popular applause for the potent root of life when, in the position of the woman who crouches on the bed in the attitude of an eastern saint at prayer, there is no discontinuity between her buttocks and her sex.

To us in Po, this never has sounded vulgar. It has always had the same meaning as *Bramosa Felice*, the joyous revelry of physical love; one of those breakthroughs into contentment with all creation that make life worth the trouble.

BETRAYAL

The evil tic that makes a woman keep on betraying everyone in her life in every way she can, is called in my region the *Mente Balina*: the vaginal brain, soiled in its obsession with carnal relations.

It's an unforgiving vice, they say, and one that can't be forgiven.

Serena was the absurd contrast of her own name. For years she had betrayed her husband, Federico, ever more shamelessly, to the point of trumpeting her falseness, spending the nights in her lovers' beds, one after the other, coming home at dawn.

Federico, who loved her deeply, had known from the beginning, endured it from the beginning. He knew that little could be done against the *Mente Balina*, except oppose it with the unheard patience of love, the hope, ripped through with pain, that a miracle might happen one day.

Every day at dawn Federico, a saddler by trade, repeated the same gestures; but each day it seemed to him that he was performing them for the first time. The as yet invisible light, getting ready to come up from behind the Donada hill, roused him like a gong, sunlight shaped into a bell, and he lifted his head from his arms, folded on the worktable where he had fallen asleep.

⧫

He saw blood-red outlines along the saddles that told him: it's time. Even the smell of leather stayed with him like a drug, sweeping his brain clean, making it quick and lucid. He took a deep breath. Then he listened. A little time passed. He had gotten used to the furtive noises Serena made when she came back from her nights spent God knows where and with whom, but each time his stomach still cramped as it had when he first realized that she was betraying him with every man she met.

He waited for his wife to go upstairs to the room at the end of the corridor where she slept alone, waited for her to wash her face and wipe off the traces of the loves she had consummated with other men. Then he left the saddlery and went upstairs himself. He wasn't inured to the emotions that came to him as he hesitated over the doorknob, turned it, with his heart suspended, knowing he would find her already in bed, with her back turned, eyes fixed on the wall. He stood beside the bed waiting patiently for Serena to turn over and try to focus on his face.

He smiled at her. She tried to smile, too, but she couldn't.

Federico sat down on the edge of the bed, stroking her hand abandoned on the coverlet. It had been a lifetime since he had asked her, "Let me lie down beside you?"

But to renounce this question, banish it from his soul, made him feel the same emptiness that he had felt that morning, now long ago, when he had felt the words die on his lips. All he did was lift his wife's chin, saying:

"Let me look in your eyes."

Serena obeyed, offering her gaze to his scrutiny.

Federico searched deeply into her lost look; he wanted to see if some light of reason, however small, still persisted in her eyes that shifted from intensest blue to green, or if the *Mente Balìna* had completely cancelled it. It was always with the terror of the first time that he insinuated his loving power of understanding between her trembling eyelids; with the delight of the first time that he saw that the light still held, no matter how far back in a corner, like a little animal crouching in the dark.

This happiness sufficed him. He kissed Serena's forehead, wished her sweet dreams, and stood up to leave.

Time had not softened the next moment, it had made it ever more tense, almost unbearable by now: would Serena say his name before he reached the door? He turned away, concentrating all his strength on placing his hand on the knob. A question of seconds, he realized; every morning his fate depended on a question of seconds. Because Serena was fighting to tell him:

"Lie down beside me. We can make love. We'll forget everything and go back to the beginning."

A lifetime, again, in which the two of them came so close to the words that moved imperceptibly on her lips. Come on, he urged her in his mind, try, Serena, you're about to say it, come on. Then the words clouded over for the tiniest fraction of a second and the *Mente Balìna* gripped her head again, making her turn away with a sob. Then Federico closed the door behind him.

He went out to look at the little hill, hoping the new sun would burn away the images that had just been engraved on his retina; that it would blind him, in his brain, in his memory, too, so that he would no longer see anything in the world, not think about anything any more. . . .

It's a photo from the nineteen-forties, printed on a postcard. On the back, space for a message and an address. But no one had ever sent it. It had remained in my mother's drawer, then in my worktable, one of my dearest and most secret things.

The snapshot has effects of light and a disposition of the figures that reminds me of Manet, with a background that tends to disappear into lights and darks, making up an indeterminate place. But it's certainly Parma with the circle of old walls, elms, horse-chestnut trees. And women chatting on benches.

Summer must be at the gates. On the left you can make out cherry trees with their white blossoms, wisteria pouring over the façades. From an arch in the city wall, barely visible, a little military band marches forth. It must be a feast day because a scrawl of Parmigiano dialect says: *Col zachèt e il braghi tiràdi*, with jacket and pants pressed with a hot iron, as for festive occasions.

The one in the foreground, there in the light, is my father. Next to him, my mother, taken by surprise, elegantly dressed. They exude the immediacy of just having met, laughter in their look, challenge in their pose, directed at whoever is capturing their image.

The whole card breathes out the limpidness of their meeting, and of the city that surrounds them. Of the harmony of their being together. It is the only image remaining to me from a family past that, to judge by my life at this particular moment, seems to belong to another person.

I found it unexpectedly in my hands as I was sorting through a pile of mail. I was stunned that someone had not only taken it out of my desk, but had even known that I had hidden it there.

And yet it happened.

And whoever took it from me had now sent it back from a town with an undecipherable postmark. Indecipherable, too, at first, the name scrawled across the back. I made a thousand guesses, then finally I understood who it was.

I thought of Silvia with enormous gratitude.

A strain of the music of life accompanied my gesture as I closed it back in the drawer where it belonged.

THE ITINERARIES OF EROS

Multi-column headlines in the papers:

"Italians romp in merry villas of Castelli Romani, sanctuaries for sin seekers. Villas of vice: group sex, isolated, by reservation only, centuries-old trees in gardens of perversion, upper floors crowded with beds. New hot business. Forget about selling D.O.C. wines and *porchetta* ... Buzz from the gate, give the password, come in and sin. Police investigate 'Culture clubs' used as cover. . . ."

Yet again, the Italy of squalor.

If the brain doesn't communicate, an obsession may be born there. So say neuropsychologists in explaining some psychotic disturbances. The diagnosis may be equally applied to today's society. The brain of this society communicates its notions of ideology, things of the spirit and culture, with ever greater difficulty; consequently, it fixates on "minor" and troubling aspects, including certain sexual practices, not experienced as the happy fruition of instinct and eroticism but as taboos for psychotic release.

It's the Italy of the personals column: "Erotomaniac seeks same."

To attract the public with ready-made scandal, pre-packaged like souvenirs of sexual eccentricity. Eros in Naugahyde, frequently plastic. The pathetic alibi of a social desperation which is itself entirely authentic, nestled in the heart of a largely bewildered multitude.

Man suffers from an historic fatigue which has borne him back into the old, repetitive formula of wanting and clumsily taking possession of a vagina. He doesn't know how to live through this fatigue, he doesn't understand its mechanisms, by instinct he conceals it ("Tangentopolis" is the perfect scenic representation of a corrupt male "fatigue"). Woman suffers from a different malady: the quest for a companion she can never find. Not finding him, she falls prey to a fixation, and then she either goes into hiding, closed and spiny as a hedgehog, and communicates with no one, or she swings to the opposite pole, which is self-degradation, throwing herself away sexually.

The drama lies in these two conflicting drives: on the one side, the thwarted psychological development of the man; on the other, the woman's deluded quest. Today the concept of hope is in decline, it is no longer the theme of the future. How can you hope in a world that has none?

Everything is confused. With collective hope dead, there remains only the individual wish: each person thinks of how to ensure his own survival, which he must learn to manage like a property, a little farm. Only if we manage to construct a network of a great many altruistic "little farms" will something be born again.

Here it is, the "Villa of vice": half-hidden in the trees, behind a stone wall, high solid wooden gates with impressive latches and bars, cascades of ivy, wisteria in the background. There is another entrance from the main road, the owner's — by profession a breeder of German shepherds — who had rented out the villa to an enterprising couple. The big white sign says: "Puppies. Reserve your heart's desire for 1994 . . ."

I read this story in *La Repubblica*: "To judge by the license plates of the luxury cars that last Saturday night filled the garden of "La Gioconda," the self-styled cultural club at Grottaferrata, where some fifty 'red-light VIP's' came not only from the capital but from much farther away, converging here from Verona, for example, from Bologna, Ravenna, Ancona. . . . Executives, entrepreneurs, lawyers. . . . Sodom and Gomorrah in this town of princely villas and papal residences. Saturday night five police agents managed to infiltrate the scene and pass for clients: two couples and a single. There followed a Boccaccioesque tale of mature gentlemen surprised in unpleasant situations, wives and girlfriends, tangles of limbs, orgies in rooms with a view, in the sense that the doors had been removed and the walls covered with mirrors; screens that multiplied pornovideos to infinity, waterbeds (the cause of so many transgressions), crowded cubicles, naked matrons on red divans, winking music, more or less premeditated stripteases. . . ."

From my "notes" on the spectacles and episodes recorded inside: the man who's weeping, sitting on a divan, ignored; a grim older man who weeps because his wife has gone up with an unknown youth to the floor above, and his weeping is disguised by an automatic lifting of his fingers, rubbing across his eyeglasses which are crooked, the lenses fogged. . . .

He would like to close out his life like a caprice that has turned into torment, a crazy mistake. He had been driven by a desire for complicity among people who feel superfluous but now he hates the fact of being among them.

≈◈

The girl moves rapidly through the room, closing windows, turning on lights. She wants the set to come to life, to come out of the shadows, to be revealed in its naked reality; and she wants this for herself, too: to come to life, to be stripped bare like the stage itself.

Francesco V., once a famous lover, now has to draw upon old licentious skills: he passes magician's hands over her body; in the gestures with which he lifts up her dress, he suddenly finds something he would never have imagined: nostalgia, in a purely affective sense, for his best years, a desperate disappointment. He understands that people like him are clowns, that amorous companions no longer want a master of ceremonies, that gallantry has waned, that nothing remains that can shock the morality of this new time, the girl is there to prove that: today there is no longer any morality to offend, scandal has worn threadbare, the present doesn't even taste like an epoch.

The girl's body, undressed now, is a fetish that attracts and at the same time derides him. Pitilessly it mirrors his breakdown as a protagonist. The man makes a gesture as if to pull her onto the bed, but in reality it's he who lets himself be pulled down, anxiously watching over his sex which — just think — long ago was famous among women. Use it, stick it in like a weapon; he has no other choice. The brutality of the act doesn't bother his casual partner; still penetrated, she slips his wristwatch off and puts it carefully on the nightstand.

The more furiously he plunges, the more Francesco V. feels ignored, superfluous, so lonely he can hardly bear it. He keeps on raging away until the girl's actions, those details, take on the strength of his desperation. When he falls across her, he stares at his own sweat which has soaked the sheets, sliding down his face, while the girl's face is tense, dry, and she's grimacing at that sweat, that semen smeared over her.

※

Marina C. had come with her boyfriend, Orlando N.

She tries to assign an identity to those around her, mature men and women, younger couples, girls. Executives, their lovers, students, shopgirls? Middle-class drones, squalid little actresses, models?

She shuts her eyes. When she opens them again, she notices a young man who seems different from the others, and she guesses that he's a foreigner: he's sitting alone, looking nice, without participating. There's a piano. From time to time Marina reaches out her hand, presses her finger against a key. With every note, a little, heartbreaking melancholy.

In the background, Orlando is kissing the breasts of . . . But now Marina sees that she herself is being assaulted, they're all over her, they poke into her like crabs. And she presses, over and over, a piano key. Until they slip away into the huge room which is a pool of half-words, muffled laughter, limp orgasms, a few shrieks: a lady has hysterics, quickly puts on her clothes, and leaves, slamming the door.

Women kneel down, pushing between Marina's legs, busying themselves with mechanical precision, with digital articulation of their lack of imagination; she feels between her knees the quickened beating of their hearts, and with an equal precision she strikes her finger on the keys again.

Orlando comes past her, scolding:

"Please don't do your usual wet blanket number."

He shuts the lid of the keyboard with a firm dry thump. She opens it again, the keyboard glows under one of the few lamps left lighted. A man stops beside her, his face dripping sweat, his fiancée beside him, and now he's contemplating her hand on the keyboard. That flicker of grace seems to enchant him. He smiles, fascinated and satisfied by nothing more than Marina's index finger which searches one note after another. Then he remembers, regretfully, the reason they're gathered there, and he's on top of her. While it lasts, the fiancée, seated on the floor a little distance away, keeps her eyes on Marina's, and Marina keeps looking into hers. The man detaches himself, and neither of them wants to be the first to look away.

A boy takes the fiancée by her arms and drags her to the other end of the room. Looking after them, Marina sees, framed in the dead field of vision, Orlando lying between two women who bend over his body. He's looking at the ceiling, perhaps he too has found a point, like a key lost in a piano: a point — she believes — containing impossible fantasy.

Among all those who are showing off their energy and improvisational skills, the young man who looks foreign and nice continues to sit quietly, his arms wrapped around his knees, where he rests his chin and watches Marina. He looks intensely at her, not to see what she's doing; indeed, ignoring that, with a serene transparency in his eyes. Only her face interests him, as if nothing were happening to her body below the shoulders.

Orlando notices and smiles sarcastically.

. . . Marina realizes that most of them are going away. She hears cars leaving, windows opening to let out the smoke that makes cloudy halos around the lamps, and the dawn air comes in to do subtle battle with the smoky clouds and halos. Orlando enters her, there where others have entered, in the bed where others have been, leaving behind their waste elements, their dead crusts. The boy concentrates on those visions, in reality it's the visions he's possessing, not the girl. They stimulate him with an excitement that makes up for something he can't identify: some emptiness, perhaps, or an anxiety, or twisted jealousy.

When Marina goes into the bathroom, she discovers that the young man who looked so nice has left a holy medal for her, wrapped up in a piece of paper on which he's traced his foreign name, hard to decipher. She comes back into the room and shows it to Orlando, holding it on her palm.

"Why does it make you so happy?" he asks her, scowling.

She tells him why: she puts all her passion and intelligence into explaining to him what fantasy is, what a gesture that expresses it means, so absolutely, so truthfully. Orlando takes the medal and squeezes it in his fist. He doesn't react as Marina feared he might.

He hesitates, drops his head, saying, "Help me. . . ."

If she didn't remember a phrase he had fiercely repeated to her ("I'm proud to say I've never cried in my life"), she would really believe that he was weeping: slowly, without letting anyone see, until his plaint took on sound and fled away, with the emptiness, the anxiety, the twisted jealousy. A weeping that sets him free.

They stay there beside each other.

NOTES IN THE MARGIN

A conversation between two woman friends
regarding certain mens' misinterpretation of Eros

Eleonora M. and Laura T. are surrounded by the violet sunset, under the spell of the color of the light which suggests a longing for lightness, for happy flight.

Eleonora looked into Laura's eyes: they were filled with the ineffable lightness of someone who'd like to float up into the air, abandoning contact with her own reality. And this pushed her to set herself free, to utter confidences. She talked about the contradictions that were tormenting Loris, her lover, and therefore tormented her, too; about how he drew her into heavily carnal situations, bringing her together with other men, other women; about all the games that didn't come out of honest emotions, even though it was he who was constructing them, and which therefore didn't even give him sexual pleasure.

These shadow barriers had spoiled a relationship that could have been beautiful, and had kept her from really being able to love him.

Eleonora said, "I envy you, Laura. You and your man have a kind of clarity together, even in the worst situations."

"I think we do," said Laura. "It depends on imagination. If you've got it and you only use it for pleasure, it can make you have feelings, it can make each of you understand you're the other's accomplice. But if you don't have it, or, worse, if you only use it when you need to push yourself into doing things that feel sick and vicious, then you lose enthusiasm for being an accomplice, and then of course it makes everything trashy."

"And what about Loris?"

"Anguish can come between us and the person we love, just like a wall; and then you try things, you invent situations to stir up at least some false excitement, so that you won't notice the wall."

"But then how do you explain his jealousy? A jealous man would never share his woman with others."

"Sometimes men obey a kind of crazy logic in their erotic behavior. Maybe they love a woman really excessively and they say: the idea that she might be unfaithful without my knowing it makes me crazy. I'm afraid of her betraying me without my knowledge; I *feel* those betrayals and then they run away, as if they were making fun of me. I'd rather be responsible for them, rather have them somehow come from me . . ."

Eleonora observed with bitter humor, "And to think I believed he was a dreamer."

"And who says he's not? A man always dreams of flying high, if he doesn't, then he doesn't feel like a man. But when he realizes he can't be as great as he's dreamed of being . . . That it would take such a little bit to get there, that he only needs to fly a tiny bit higher, but he just can't do it . . ."

Eleonora interrupted her. "In fact, he was so close to being the right man for me. That's what makes me so angry."

The other went on: "That tiny unbridgeable gap that separates him from being happy, depresses him, makes him humiliate himself and you, wanting to destroy and be destroyed, rolling around in the manure pit. And remember: in a man's soul there's always a dark background of hate for a woman, even when he loves her . . ."

"Love is really complicated, eh?"

"I'd say so. And so is Eros."

"Maybe I made a mistake. I shouldn't have done all the things he wanted. I shouldn't have."

Laura surprised her, explaining, "But you weren't doing them to please him. You do it because you see it as a way of thanking him."

Eleonora felt amazed, but she nodded.

"You're grateful for the happiness you have when you're together in the way you know you should be."

"That's true. And it's such a strange happiness. I do feel it when I'm with him, right, because those are the times he's really gentle and passionate, but I have the sensation that it's not coming from him . . . Maybe I'm crazy. Or maybe I'm paying for mistakes, like when I used to throw myself away on a bunch of idiots. And you — remember? — you warned me: 'you're wasting too much anger on men, on the world, too much spite for yourself, too . . .' You were right. And you end up by yielding, wasted, just to have a little peace, even if you have to pay for it later."

"No, Eleonora, of course you're not crazy. Go on, stay with him, just don't shut your eyes to what he's really like — I think that's slipping away from you now.

"Reassure him, help him, you need to be as patient as, I don't know, a mother, so he can make that next little flight and grow up, be an adult . . . Men are like that.

"And often it's not even their fault. Often they're children who know they're children, who are deeply hurt by this, who have too many women around them incarnating their mother, women who've given themselves to too many men, for their pleasure, to too many *fathers*, and it's this that makes them feel somehow orphans."

"And haven't they gone with a hundred women? Don't they still?"

"Of course. But nature lets children go unpunished for being cynical and greedy, because they don't yet know anything about life. And so they think their souls aren't involved, and that's probably true: their childishness in love lets them get away with that. But it's up to us to understand them, because we're the ones who have, always and ever more, a restlessness in our hearts that they don't know about. . . . It's useless to say: if you do it, I'm going to do it too. Our destiny, however thankless and unfair, is that we're amorously superior . . ."

THERE EXISTS AN EROS OF FAREWELL, OF ENDINGS

When a story ends, you think of particulars, of the smallest episodes. These bloom out of what once had been the ordinary, and now they seem to be of the most overwhelming beauty. It's the details, much more than their context: gestures, sentences, an embrace under a streetlight, and each remembered detail becomes so vivid: that light, that moment of human contact when it seemed that nothing, no one, could ever break that perfect thing.

A wound has been opened. Time has to sew its edges back together. A recurrent thought: "Why do things have to end like this?"

These details of Eros surge back with such enormous potency, assailing you with painful desire.

There are moments in which the idea that she's having pleasure with another man is unbearable. The thorn in the senses pricks the imagination: as if she were possessed of an enormous erotic power, which you took for granted before. And now it seems to you like a vast delight that she's bestowing on men you don't know, and from which you are excluded forever. Including — as I've already had occasion to say — those *teachings*, all those things you gave her. When will the wound close up? When will this jealousy, this suffering that's so different from all others, end?

The regret will cease, the regret for an Eros who belonged to you and who now seems to have flown away into the possession and realm of outsiders, but you will notice that your life has used up part of the time allotted to it by fate. What's left is a hole, a chasm which you may be able to fill, but which nonetheless makes you feel closer to death.

In the meantime, you urgently want to possess all those details, sending the time machine back into the past:

. . . You see certain images again: as when she was getting dressed beside the bed. The room was dark. But the window let a square of white light come through the drawn curtains and rest on the wall, the light of a summer dawn announcing the bright day.

You used to love that moment, before she left your house, while in the shadows of her face the lineaments, the shapes, the expressions began to surface, as if they were being born out of a neutral background of nonexistence, like to the idea she was leaving with you, the desire to tell it on the written page. You would sit in front of the blank page and you had to give features, form, expressions to this idea with the same illuminating processes as the dawn.

Before she began to dress, she would move her hands over her body to take possession of it again, preparing it for the battles of the coming day which she had forgotten during the night of love. She appeared to you as a warrior preparing herself, calculating her strength, and for just a few moments she seemed uncertain: she thought it would be nice to stay there with her stocking half on, posed like a figure in a painting, her fingers holding its upper edge just above her knee, her foot resting on a chair, the naked body bent casually forward, yet visibly showing a perplexity that changed into time suspended.

All night she had held you in her arms, tightly, against the world of other people . . .

Go back and read the letters that she wrote you.

Someone of a romantic sensibility might tell a friend how he used to write letters to a woman he loved, sending them from one room to the other of the hotel suite where they were taking a brief vacation from the world.

"From room to room?"

"Of course; they were love letters, and love doesn't recognize distances even when they exist. And so the idea was to send them to her from nearby. I would get up at dawn, I'd close myself in the living room with my paper and pen, and then I'd slip the envelope under the bedroom door. She found it when she woke up."

She might read:

"I love savoring Paris with you. Among all the priceless moments, I'll remember walking with you on the boulevards, and that there were benches here and there, and you sat down, a little bit tired, and I sat beside you, I put my arm around your shoulders, sharing your happy exhaustion, and the setting sun that warmed your back . . . Paris is a city that you put on like a wedding dress. Does it really matter if you marry or if you discover that marriage was a game?"

And also:

"Last night in that nightclub we listened to an old Charles Trenet song *Y a d'la joie! . . . There's joy! . . .* yes, joy does exist, I know it now, with you."

Another letter, written aboard a ship sailing to America:

"When you turned and saw that we were leaving Europe behind, I was so happy to read in your eyes the pleasure you were feeling . . . It's like turning your head from the reality of a moment ago and seeing the ocean light that changes everything . . . And you burst into delighted laughter, because the ocean took your breath away with its immensity, but also because you could see a little cloud overhead that was just like the one that greeted you every morning of your childhood, floating over the house where you were born. All the passengers were magnetized by you, and thanks to you I felt so many things belonged to me: the ship sailing out triumphantly, your body, your memory, contentment from some trifling thing; the ocean. . . ."

Other letters. Other voyages.

The high plateaus of Asia, the purple roses of the Nile, Japan's imperial gardens, impertinent embraces stolen in front of the sleeping Buddha (or was he only pretending?). The high seas where only fabled and daring explorers had gone, where we made love on little boats in the exact places where extraordinary events took place in the books we had read as passionate children, dreaming of adventure . . .

One of the last letters said:

"Eros is your being, my magic flute brimming with music no other artist could play. In Mozart's *Magic Flute*, too, what vast material: comic scenes, dramatic passages, fabulous rites of initiation and endless wanderings, witchcraft, ecstasy. For me this is the peak of all musical genius . . . And you, my Eros, my enchanted flute, must be kissed and held against my lips, caressed with all the devotion of my knowing fingers, enclosed in my hand for a little while, and then placed in your case, which is memory, like flame-red velvet . . . And I set this down, and your lips conserve its harmonies, as the flute still keeps the harmony of the soloist's lips.

"This is how we are, you and I."

≈

And the friend asks, "And now?"
"Now? No idea. I really don't know what became of her."

≈

There are women whose Eros won't let them stop talking, those whom ancient Chinese poets might have sung as *come from the cloudy moon which enchantment dissolves to empty sky. . . .*

I've learned that I have to detest them, avoid them. It's crucially important to recognize them at first impact, using a sixth sense which men in general do not have. They are capable of breaking off from one moment to the next. Even after the most beautiful night of love. They are excited precisely by the subtle cruelty of bringing down the curtain with a bang, of earnestly twisting the blade. And their victims are made to endure such final dialogues as the following, for no reason:

"I see you as a stranger."

He sees her, on the contrary, as more than ever familiar.

"Say something. React."

He can't. What can he say? His heart feels crushed, it seems to him that he's just heard something that makes no sense.

"When I tried to imagine this moment," she goes on, "I thought it would hurt so much. Why don't I feel anything?"

Her look is carefully vacant: "It's as if our time together had never happened. Is it possible for so much reality to be wiped out, just like that, without a trace?"

He still doesn't believe it. She seizes his arm and presses on: "Help me to feel something, at least! . . . If you don't say anything, that means that you're glad, too, deep down, glad I'm getting out of your way."

The man can't make any connection. He asks himself anxiously if the pleasure they shared meant nothing, or did it even exist? Meanwhile he hears,

"You knew this would happen sooner or later."

"No. No, I didn't know."

"Of course you did, so don't try to accuse me of being unfair."

"When?"

"Don't tell me you didn't even have a hint?"

"No. And then, tonight, even tonight, we were so . . . "

"Weren't we? But now I want it to end, right now, like this. People change. Maybe one day I'll stop changing. One day, who knows, I might get married. I'll have children. It'll be fine . . . So. I leave you with your habits, your sick interest in women who are all alike."

Months go by, every once in a while he hears news about this woman he had loved.

He hears she's had a child by someone else.

It's terrible.

EROS AND MY MOTHER AND FATHER

For my mother, time is something different. I can arrive there, right this minute, at our house in Po, and see the light shining on my dinner. She'll say: sit down, it's ready. As if I had just stepped out of the house.

Once I sat down after a long absence. We had dinner. Then I said to her: "I'd like to know how everything happened the day or the night I was conceived. I've always wondered." My mother replied with perfect naturalness:

"Then take me up to the meadows, there by Bocca di Ganda. There's a nice melon stand there now. We can eat watermelon."

I did take her to the meadows of Bocca di Ganda.

Thick darkness beyond the lights of the melon stand. Dogs were barking. We stopped at a grassy hollow that was still there, intact. It was still a place where two lovers could lie down and make love. Among the dogs and poplars. And there's an embankment which it's still possible to manage on a motor scooter.

My mother walked down into the hollow. She moved her right foot back and forth over a certain spot. She explained to me, simply, that it happened just after dark. In the afternoon it had poured rain. But it had stopped at five, and then a fiery sunset came and dried the grass. She had waited there, and my father arrived on his motorbike to keep their appointment.

A question of hours. If it had kept raining for a few more hours, I wouldn't be here now. I would have been saved from life.

EROS AND THE BROTHERHOOD OF ALL CREATURES

There is a common loneliness among living creatures.

I'm alone tonight. And my tomcat is alone, no less thirsty for love than I. He is motionless, staring at a fixed point in the dark outside, through the open window. From time to time, suddenly, he'll come over and scrape my hand with his tongue, just as he does when he's asking me to help him; if I try to strike a match, his yellow eyes draw in the flame with Luciferine avidity.

I listen, attentively. The silence is torn by the lament of a female cat in heat. She's crouching at the base of a tree in the street below. I can't think about anything else: I know I should bring her up here and let her be with my cat. It wouldn't be hard to pick her up. Until a few years ago, I managed to coax much more dangerous animals within reach, touch them, hold them. Big game hunters admired my skill.

I think a bag should do it. I take one down to the street, I know I can entice her in. And so it comes to pass.

The female slides plumply along the wall and is already in our bedroom, she hisses, showing her little fangs, she has a poor ugly

chopped-off tail and has been bitten by dogs; she comes close to
my cat and suddenly bounces back, arching; my cat waits, decides:
he sniffs her from a distance, he sniffs her from nearby, he sniffs
along her body.

There comes a moment in which both of them are standing on
their hind paws, using the others to climb the air, full throat against
full throat, and their amorous play begins.

At which point I retire.

I close the door and leave them to the felicity of the game they
play so well.

EROS AND SECRET WRITINGS

Whoever has an authentic devotion to Eros writes about it: an ordinary diary, often kept hidden, ciphered notes, almost a secret and
personal code, scribblings in a notebook, mixed in with reminders
of things to do in the course of the day. This happens when the
meanings of Eros intermingle with the habits and customs of a life.

The great poets of Eros have all kept a diary. Pages of great
sweetness, followed by other, terrible, pages.

I, too, find myself looking for things I've written on scattered
sheets, hidden here and there. . . .

There are instances, tiny episodes, discoveries that for me were
extraordinary. Nothing is invented. For the most part I write in the
heat of the moment, still possessed by my emotions, wanting to live
them again immediately afterwards in perspective, placing them
within the story of my life. I think that it will be possible for me to
reread my life one day, as an old man, and this idea delights me, excites me once again, gives back to me the scent of someone else's

skin on mine, my eyes aglow with the light of other eyes. It will be beautiful to savor passion once again, through memory.

The images, the words, the inventions of lovers, the silences, the orgasms, the little madnesses, all become the heart-throbbing sinuosity of writing itself.

Erotic charm is always luminous, radiant, it shouldn't be allowed to dwindle away. Let nothing be lost of that precious property. Going through my pages — the ones I manage to find, many having been lost — allows me to see myself once more in the days and events of my youth, wiping out the years, with the pleasure of having enjoyed my part in them. That's the point: the pleasure of reading the pleasures I have been granted, that I achieved in harmony with nature which, even more than ourselves, yearns not to be bored. Of course a certain melancholy comes with it. But why see this as negative? Isn't that the very sensibility that pushes us into poetry, into fiction?

I come across names, dates. *That* day . . . Among all the more or less distant loves, I meet again "the most astonishing," "the women of my voyages," "leading ladies," "the jealous ones," "the most intelligent," "the mysterious," and so on. Besides revelations and confessions, I also find details of behavior. Delights and abasements. Moments of genius in chamber music; duets, tercets, extravagant equivocations, a commitment to making the most of bows, pizzicati, tremolos, mutes.

Music . . . my list as its score. As Eros is.

Notes, unlike words, desire us, as we desire them. They are the double mirror of our desire.

Dear loves of my scrawled pages: sometimes it all seemed so fugitive. We were together around the clock, so that we never noticed how we fooled ourselves. And now, something of us risks lasting throughout time.

My exchanges with A. B. continue, in her house outside Rome, across from a greenhouse where no flower has been forgotten: from the humblest ones of field and roadside to every species of rose and orchid. I admit to her:

"I've never cared much for the professions of faith of famous libertine writers. The cult of their *ars amandi* usually sounds spoiled, self-indulgent; using Eros' stage directions to salvage a carnal soul they don't possess. Eros really can't fall into cerebration or intellectual and didactic schemes."

"What do you mean by libertine?"

"What Madame de Maintenon meant when she used it for '*dissolute*,' someone whose behavior is out of bounds, irregular. But be careful: the false libertine, in literature, really does regulate, and in a rather captious way, the performance of misrule. He invents and directs its every tiny detail. But life's authentic libertine doesn't know a thing about these codified forms, not even when he picks up a pen."

"And some of these writings bother you?"

"They don't just bother me, they ravish me, overwhelm me, transport me with their immediacy, horrify me sometimes, but they never give me the least hint of artifice . . . I'm talking about those courageous, or anyway certainly not literary, persons who consign themselves to secret pages like the message in a bottle that the castaway entrusts to the sea, to chance. Without once asking himself if it isn't most likely to end up bobbing against some wrecked hulk. Here's another metaphor with the same elements: I love those who write about Eros, using their pages just as compulsively as someone who builds a miniature ship inside yet another bottle, which is itself a symbol of the carnal sortilege to which our origin is linked, with primordial evocations and perversities. While the boat symbolizes the writer, who has imprisoned himself in that mystery."

A. B. keeps a secret diary, I know.

I continue: "I love that filigreed depravity, with a goldsmith's touch. People involved in the body's festive rites, or, on the contrary, in dramas and tragedies that frequently fill up headlines on the crime page. They put their lives at risk, with the gusto of Rabelais or the desperation of Céline. They're dissolute not because of licentiousness, but because they're really not afraid of disappearing into their seductive or terrifying needs. . . ."

"Give me some examples."

"I could tell you about the Marchese Casati and some others like him. Or the diaries that women keep bringing me, with no intention of having them published, just because they see me as their daylight accomplice, someone who can save them from sinking into the shadows of their sexual bondage, into abjection, into their own cruelty. In all these pages there is a *something* . . . however it may be expressed, a thrilling narrative strength. At which point psychology and psychopathology can be used as a screen against which we read other significations of life today, beyond the lives of sex."

It was one of the most shocking tragedies of postwar Rome. A disturbing case about which, in a city usually apathetic even about crime, rumors have never ceased to grow.

1970. Via Puccini 9. The bodies are discovered the night of August 30. The Marchese Camillo Casati Stampa di Soncino committed suicide after killing his wife, Anna Fallarino, forty-one years old, still extremely beautiful, and Massimo Minorenti, twenty-four, who had a stormy political history as an activist of the extreme right, the son of a good Roman bourgeois family and known, as we read in the police report, "as being attractive and attracted to women."

The case was speedily closed as a triple drama of jealousy, involving a family at the very height of aristocracy, with a fortune including countless billions, many palaces, the island of Zanone in the Ponza archipelago, the villa at Arcore now owned by Silvio Berlusconi, and a rich tradition from the Risorgimento (Gabrio Casati was president of the provisional government that came out of the Cinque Giornate).

It was the marchese himself who introduced his wife to young Massimo, promising him her favors and presiding over their concession. An intense three-way relationship was born out of this and lasted for some time. Camillo Casati usually promoted erotic games with several people, the better to attend his wife's performances: many personages of Roman high society and the nobility sported with the marchesa.

The drama begins when Anna Fallarino and Massimo Minorenti fall in love. Casati realizes that the two are eluding his control, discovers that they are meeting secretly, and that he has been banished from their sexual relations. He goes crazy. He can't accept his new rôle as a bit player after having been the director of what was intended to remain a carnal comedy. He feels "betrayed" at last.

His homicidal fury explodes. A note is found in which the marchese writes, before killing himself, "I'm dying because I can't bear your loving another man." In whatever twisted, paradoxical, sick ways, he had always loved his wife Anna, even as he subjected her to multiform acts of perversion; and so profound was his bond with her that in the face of her "betrayal" the depraved Casati fell to pieces even more quickly than men who discover similar outrages after a life of what are called normal relations.

This is one of the cases that make one reflect on the dark connections between sexual pathology and the affective life.

Camillo Casati was obsessed with setting down, by means of camera and pen, the moments and attitudes of his erotic complicity with Anna.

He wrote the overwhelming *Green Diary*, of which the police seized only a part. Its pages contain secrets and annotations about an entire society striated with depravity. In this sense, some passages are memorable. However, the authorities, the press, and those who had occasion to review it were especially excited by a single excerpt. This yields yet another proof of the mundane and morbid taste of the so-called "non-depraved" element:

". . . This year at Ischia, after a night of kisses with one of our woman friends, [Anna's] labia majora had become large and swollen, and, understanding that Anna, although she said nothing, was dying to show off, I took her down to a deserted beach where she could perfectly well wait, naked, for eventual passersby. At a certain point five boys (18–22 years old) appeared, all habitués who knew that nude foreign women often came there; Anna stretched out on the air mattress with her legs apart; naturally the boys stopped, and pretended that they just happened to be passing, buzzing around us: when they saw that we weren't going to react they came closer and stared. Her labia really were enormous, almost double their normal size. After a good five minutes Anna told them not to move and not to touch her, but just to look at her because that was what she desired. She began to touch herself, first with one hand, then with both; masturbating for at least a quarter of an hour, and she came when the boys, standing there, touching themselves, almost all came at the same time. But she hadn't touched any of them nor had they touched her.

"For myself, erotically, it's all fine . . . I'm not a homosexual, but I can't say I mind the presence of another man."

The diary of N., involved in a strange Emilian scandal: She was an ambitious little performer who tried acting in every medium — film, theatre, television — but most of all, in her own cruelty. In the pages she wrote, mostly about her relations with a famous director, the cruelty of the banal flows along without pause or light:

" . . . He treated me like a star, at least that's how it seemed to me. He sent a car to pick me up, he put my photo up on the wall of the office and he said my face was so innocent, it made him have to be serious . . . Then one day, in the afternoon, we made love. He kissed me, he touched my breasts, so I took off my clothes. I really did it because he was old. And I thought, 'I'm not going to find another one his age. I'm curious to see how an old guy makes love!' . . . "

This is a mode of non-being, of repeatedly leaving on others the marks of cynicism described with an absence of alibis and justifications that is so absolute as to make the sincerity of the confession frightful. I read many, too many, diaries like this: their number grows daily.

There are many, too many, personages like the famous director and the dreary girl.

I recall my friend Piero with great affection. Eros had united us in a common sentiment, even in those moments which people of ill will call transgressions but which I know express a nobility of the heart.

I often reread the pages of his journal: this one, for example, the last. And it always moves me. And again I find myself mirrored in my friend. It's Piero's farewell to the woman he had lived with, loving her in spite of everything:

". . . My life appears to me as an uninhabitable void. It's the empti-ness of a theatre to which neither actors nor audience will ever re-turn. You used to scold me: 'You want to live everything all at once.' It's true, but not in the sense you believed. I never degraded myself, I was never a whoremaster, as you called me. If I got inside women's lives — even cruel ones, because you women don't notice how much you hate one another — it was to understand their mode of being, always, however, with a paradoxical respect. As if I were cu-rious about a tree. About a light. Suppose there's a light at the win-dow. I look at that lighted window, and I see that it's different from the others, I feel an irresistible need to know about the life that's going on inside that unknown room. A regret (absurd, I know) that that mystery has to escape me.

"You kept on reproving me. Rightfully, from your point of view. I did try. I renounced my curiosity, closing myself up in the house for days. At the end it was suffocating us. A priceless pleasure was disappearing: ubiquity. Yes, I did need to be everywhere at once; just as I needed to be able to lose myself suddenly in other, differ-ent lives, while keeping the joy of rushing back into your solar light . . . I've always known I would be as abject as a thief if I ever falsely told a woman 'I love you.' I've had friends who were very skilled at saying it, lying; like riding a motorcycle on one wheel. But what about some women's 'I love you'? Give them a few orgasms and here it comes, immediately after their cry of pleasure, they emit an 'I love you!'

"Sincerely, I have said those words only to you. I want you to know this. And you know it's true. Men in general, dear friend, only respect the failures they themselves provoke. For them, ideally, women should be mediocre. I've never thought you were mediocre. I've never known a mediocre woman . . . And now? Losing me, what risks is your dogmatism going to run in this slaughterhouse world that destroys those qualities whose grace is an insult to their miserable ragings? How many of the debts I paid for you, to shelter you from the world, will come back to burden you when I'm no longer there to shield you from the blows?

"I beg you to forgive me. It's best that I get out of the way: your way, mine. Some time will go by, and then — and I tremble at this thought — you may go back to throwing yourself away on a different man every night, like those squalid and greedy wretches you used to know.

"You thought you could control them and everything that happened between you. But it was they, the day after, who filed you away under 'whore' . . . It's the thought of this that's destroying me. I've never classified anyone as a whore. Always, however it was, a sentiment of gratitude illuminated me.

"I'm glad that the *time of women* has ended for me, forever. What a horrible contrast between the verb '*godere*'[2], which once meant *gaudio*, a holy celebration, but is now used with automatic vulgarity, and the falsities, the contortions, the too frequent torment it requires!

"Please take care of my cat. She was a part of me. And she will continue to be in your new life . . . "

I haven't heard from Piero for a long time. The last time I saw him was when he came to leave his diary with me.

I miss him.

How many men there are, indeed, who are Piero's exact opposite. And I hate them with my whole being. I'll take one at random, among all the ones described to me as symbols of those who taint the world of relationships between male and female. The diary of B., aged thirty, tells of a prototype who enjoys a certain banal notoriety and is considered a comic actor; of the comic spirit,

2. 'to achieve orgasm', from the Latin *gaudere*.

however, which should always be like one of the angels painted by Correggio, with the wit that informs flesh with the glow of joy, he possesses only the blackened skeleton, a cherub's skeleton, and a presumptuous mimetic tic, intimately lugubrious.

Eros has never brushed the slightest grace over him. He is among the vain men, mediocre even in their vanity, who use vaginas to act out their complexes of inferiority. Through women, too, they vent the anguish that gnaws them: they will never, not even for an instant, be authentic creative talents. This kind of man is like an orangutan in the zoo. And yet women swarm to them. Even women who are not obviously stupid. They make up reasons, but there can be no reason. "A seal of approval," they say, trying to joke about it. But that's still horrible. Why, then? Why be gratified by foolish notoriety? It's hard to understand, hard even to feel pity, comprehension.

B.'s diary is saved at least by the honesty and repugnance she expresses with such force:

"... He drinks another glass, then jumps on me. He takes off his clothes, takes off mine, it all happens in a blink. He looks over at me and says, 'You've got a great ass.' He pulls me into the bedroom. He brings his bottle. He takes another drink, and then he pours it over me and starts licking me like an ice-cream cone. He enters me, and I can't say it's a pleasure ... he takes me into the bathroom. He sets me on the washbasin, against the mirror. I'm propped there on the sink as he takes me with his arrogant member, rotten drunk: 'Look at you, you're so beautiful.' I don't enjoy his sex, so presumptuous and hasty, but it offers me a conscious image of myself ... I go to Rome with him. Before he fucks me he sings songs to me, plays the guitar. I accept his prick, pickled in alcohol. And then he's eager to please, grateful, proud. He's carved another notch on his blade ... His tacky plastic world attracts me, but all he wants me for is that ... He drinks, he smokes, he can't do it unless he's slopping over with drink ... All this scares me because I'm resigned to it. I leave, disgusted. I'm crying my heart out, feeling it grow colder and colder.

"I feel an irresistible desire to vomit up all that's female in me, kill it. I don't have the faintest idea of what a real orgasm might be. And of all the men who have stuck themselves into my womb, not one has known how to say one human thing to me, forget about anything erotic. I've never cried out, but from time to time I make a weak little whimper that's supposed to mean Thanks, is it over? . . . Thank you thank you for your dangling, useless, dumb appendage, whose dull torture I endure in the hope of finding some lousy gesture of affection."

B.'s diary deserves to be published and widely circulated; it's a testament which reveals an unusual aspect of the female confrontation with male imbecility.

I hope that B. is not lost, with no hope of rescue, in her desperation, in her bewilderment.

HAPPINESS GREAT AND SMALL . . .

. . . Daydreaming, I rise up high, so high, in fantasy: there where astronomers now say someone up there loves someone else. . . .

Even the stars, the celestial bodies, make love.

The latest discovery comes from Japan: there even exists a "stellar birthing room," suspended between constellations in which new stars are born and formed. There were nine in the most recent nativity. This cradle in the stratosphere is, oddly, hosted by the constellation Taurus, the Bull.

The current language of cosmology speaks with affectionate

irony of "stellar sperm," of a "stellar orgasm." The Big Bang would be an example of this, a boundless echo.

. . . And so there I am, immersed in the map of the star-crowded sky, almost as if I were a part of infinite systems, as if I were breathing with their very breath. I listen intently to the silence of the celestial vault, because this silence, too, which communicates and speaks, warns us that there exists up there a language that expresses us: we are that language . . . Andromeda, the gentlest lover among all the constellations . . . It's as if I were pressing my ear against a mysterious door, and I seem to hear the sounds of the stars in the immensity of their union.

The cry of a star, a little star, barely more than a flash of light, inside a pure contour of harmonies, seems the invocation of a woman's pleasure, seems human, so human.

In my bed, in my little room, tangled in my blankets, sometimes I could hear my parents having intercourse in the next room. Those whispers, those muffled cries, first of all freed me from my fear of the dark. I used to get up, my heart trembling as I reached the closed door. I would lean against the wood, pressing lightly with my hands, my forehead, and I would keep on listening, not out of morbid interest, but with deep emotion, and I would thank God . . .

The world had not yet done anything to hurt me.

My mother, however, had already fallen victim to her depression. Her head was crowded with the sick thoughts which for years destroyed her life and ours.

I listened to her making love, and in my simple child's perception, happiness rose up in my heart for her, overcame me. That happiness for my mother, for her rare moments of joy, carried me wandering through the nighttime house. I knew that when she finished, in that hush of tired locusts which comes upon lovers afterwards, as it does to trees at twilight in the intense days of summer, my father would start to smoke, putting an azure haze around his uptilted profile, staring at the ceiling.

And that felicity pushed me to open the most secret window, to make sure that the stars, in fact, were shining upon the sleep of my happily exhausted mother.

≫

Walking through the Roman night, I tell a friend about walking through a Parma that had this same silence, the silence of nocturnal seaports, among boats at anchor, savoring it with a dolphin's playfulness, sensing that dark passageways ended in wrecked vessels instead of gardens, that the windows were scrutinizing me like the portholes of sunken ships, and that the lampposts of black iron were anchors caught in crusts of algae.

I ended up under the balcony that catches the moonlight on the façade of the hotel where I usually stay when I go to visit my mother. It was, I explain to my friend, the Bastardella's house, and I tell her about Leopold Mozart who, in a letter from Bologna in March of 1770, wrote:

"In Parma we made the acquaintance of a singer, and we went to hear her at her house, which gave us great pleasure. She is the famous Bastardella, who possesses a beautiful voice, well-placed and with incredible extension. She sang, in our presence, the notes and passages that I enclose here."

And so, standing there beneath the little balcony, that dolphin gaiety surged up like a capriole to interrupt my sedate pacing, and I imagined Leopold, who came out and announced to a little crowd, in his son's name as well, that Parma now had and would always boast, as no other city could, a powerful musical enchantress.

Then, behind his father, the adolescent Mozart appeared. They both made way, presenting La Bastardella who began to sing . . .

History reports that "La Bastardella was as talented as she was generous with her favors."

It pleases me to speculate about one of Mozart's earliest carnal emotions.

≈

When I'm feeling really down, I go to see Maurizio.

Among the friends and companions of my youthful pleasures — and call this boastful if you must, but also bear in mind that we were really good at making fun of the world — Maurizio was the opposite of Piero: witty, a genius at inventing and executing games and jokes. Idolizing Rossini, he always brings zeal and style to interpreting Eros as a great comic opera.

His amorous experiences seem to have been invariably inspired by the works of his favorite composer. Until his divorce from an unbearable wife, he paid his installments on *La cambiale di matrimonio* (*The Marriage Contract*); he wooed heavenly women by climbing athletically up *La scala di seta* (*The Silken Stair*) of their dreams; his lovers subjected him to *L'inganno felice* (*The Happy Deception*), nonetheless he saw the feminine universe, even at its worst, as *La pietra del paragone* (*The Touchstone*) of life; he never let an occasion go by, insisting, with Rossinian egoism, that *L'occasione fa il ladro* (*The Occasion Makes the Thief*); nor did he neglect any *Cenerentole* (*Cinderellas*); he lost his head over *Italians in Algiers* and *Turks in Italy*; and amiably let himself be robbed by *Gazze ladre* (*Thieving Magpies*).

He takes enormous pleasure in telling his friends about his always astonishing and eccentric adventures, as if he's never met a woman who had the slightest grip on reality. He loves these performances. What an actor! How many times Maurizio has shown off for me — I know he does it just to make me smile, and I'm always fascinated by his stories which are full of childish delight, kaleidoscopic images, and where even the most aggressive sexuality has the playful quality of children who exaggerate the world and life into giants and ogres, because fear and regret may take hold of us at any moment, leaving us nothing that really belongs to us.

Maurizio is a peerless collector and bibliophile, fascinated by everything that bears witness to the history of Eros through the centuries.

When I come to his house he welcomes me with a wink and a quotation from Pierre Masson: "For most women, *Constance* [constancy] is the name of that lake whose limpid waters bathe four different countries." As for me, I have to close my eyes, as must happen to the women my friend brings here for the first time and who are promptly stunned. For Maurizio lives within walls that are literally papered over with images of women of easy virtue, reproduced in every form and format: naughty postcards from the turn of the century, photographic nudes and illustrations from every possible provenance, erotic paintings, antique miniatures from the most diverse civilizations, prints, bookplates, lithographs, advertising figurines, cartoons.

There are authentic treasures. Such as the Japanese scrolls of Kyosai, the "Mirages of the Eastern Gardens" which were the gems of the Pasha. The walls blind one with their explosion of color wherein float, filling every space, immodest offers, suggestive poses, promises of pleasure transmitted in the form of delectable messages.

Before falling asleep, my friend looks around, closing his eyelids over retinas that still bear the luminous imprint of the multicolored nudes in this house which is one of the kingdoms of Eros, investigated as if with a telescope.

Stretching out happily, he murmurs:

"Until tomorrow, my darling friends. If ever I fall asleep without anticipating the joy of seeing you tomorrow, they'll find me dead in this bed."

I believe no detail in any book or catalogue escapes him.

The only object his collection lacks is *St. Thomas' Finger*, and this gives him no peace. He often hurries me into the Roman church of Santa Croce in Gerusalemme where, in the chapel dedicated to St. Helena, a relic of inestimable value is preserved: the very finger of St. Thomas, the one which the diffident apostle, patron of sceptics, poked between Jesus' ribs to ascertain that it was indeed He, arisen.

And Maurizio brings me close to the case in which a sapphire glows, and there, at the center, the little black shining claw stands out. Along the nail, a rust-colored rim which could be the divine blood:

"See it?" he points. "Look at it. That's the finger whose loss must make shaking hands in Heaven so awkward for the second of my patron saints, the first of course being Gioacchino Rossini."

"And so?" I say punctually, for the pleasure of hearing his explanation.

"And so remember: the finger of St. Thomas and his divine doubt is what you need to use with every kind of woman: young, old, tall, dwarf, blonde, brunette, redhead, bald, hunchbacked. As soon as you meet her, as soon as you notice you have a weakness for her, it's time to poke it in, just as the holy saint did. Otherwise you'll find your thumb stuck someplace else, and I ask the apostle to pardon me for joking about it, but, hey, he didn't respect Jesus enough to keep his hands off Him, so why should I have to be careful of his finger?"

I remind him, "Whenever you've been madly in love, it's always been with a woman who finally destroyed you."

Maurizio flung a last glance at the finger which had eluded his collection.

"True. But by choice. I always understood immediately. But I was crazy about them, and I'd tell myself: what do I care if she destroys me? Anyway, I know from the outset, and while it lasts I'm crazy with joy . . . I'm sorry, are you getting upset?"

"No, no. Not a bit."

We come out of the church, and Maurizio goes into the "Do you remember" mode.

"We've had some times, eh, D'Artagnan?" I've never understood why he calls me D'Artagnan, and I've never asked, but I like it. "Remember when . . . ?"

"Please," I try to stem the flow, because the "Remember whens" are endless. "Of course I remember, I remember everything."

But he's inspired now, he doesn't hear me.

"Remember those nights at Ostia? . . . Do you remember the princess and the peenie? Venus and the penis? . . . And Carlina who was wittier than we were, she learned all our games and played some of her own with us. Who knows whatever happened to Carlina . . . ? Do you remember the jokes we used to play? We were completely free of complexes, masters of our hearts and bodies, and clean even when we were doing something wrong, because even during the worst things, the great Gioacchino's *Ecco ridente in cielo* (*Behold the heavenly laughter*) was in our thoughts . . . We understood life so well that we could make up a pantomime, a burlesque parody of all those predictable ceremonies, so full of anxiety and conceit, that the whole horde of *coglioni* thinks it has to use to get a woman into bed . . . For four bumps and a hole, lads, a hole, because they don't see or feel anything else, they'll go through a litany fit for a coffin with the candles lit . . . What a gloomy, sinister collection of balls . . ."

I let Maurizio rave on. Also because, in such moments, he flings out his arms and quotes verses of mine that he likes:

Of us now there is hardly a heartbeat.
The evening's calm because the wind has fallen.
I make love to you
Like the carpenter, whistling so innocently,
Planing his wood.

Today at Maurizio's house, his most recent acquisition: a huge poster of *Cybersex*. This is a machine which, according to its inventors, allows one to make love at a distance, to a person who's far away. My friend explains to me that it was introduced last week at the third Salon of Eroticism in Bologna: *Erotica 94*, in the austere reaches of the convention center, and in that hellish bedlam someone had tried to get a little girl to try it out, there under the red lights. I peer at its black hood, a shiny and futuristic tangle of thermal chips, sensors, vibrators, straps, cords.

People shouted "Clowns! Buffoons!" but an enormous public curiosity was noted, with impressive, "even menacing" crowds, according to the papers, hundreds of people in line, traffic jams on the Tangenziale road. On the other hand, the porno industry, including female robots, is wildly prosperous: every year the Italians spend 1500 billion lire on pornographic merchandise and 1000 billion for hard core videos.

Maurizio kicks a hole through the poster. He picks up a newspaper and reads aloud, "Cyber, the realm of ambiguity. Input of Big Brother on politics, sex, and imagination. From virtual reality to cultural and anthropological mutation. Toward a world that opens up the path to cyberfeminism. Post-democracy: political and sexual consensus created by media of the future."

He asks me: "Do you think Italy is going to change some day? This Italy where 'being breaks down into filthy viscera,' as Gadda said. . . . Gadda, a writer I love almost as much as Rossini. What a prophet! He spoke of Italy as a mess of rotten food, a pot full of broth where they're all stewing — the bureaucracy, the ruling class, the judges and the judged, politicians and victims of politics, the true corrupters and the corrupt . . . An Italy, he said, 'powdered with anguish,' 'viscera of teratocephalics and rickety dunces,' 'idiots who cling together even in sex,' where the loss of any sense of limitation and of the ridiculous is 'gargled,' choked in the throat, it's a mass gargle . . . Will it change some day?"

We go out onto the terrace. It's the first time I see my friend's Rossinian verve diminished. He clutches other newspapers in his fist, throwing them to the wind after having read other headlines: "Farewell intimacy. Sex becomes happening," "'Porn star wanted': thousands of men and women answer ad. All eager for red light screen test. Willing to work without pay."

We stare at the fog over Rome. It's useless to turn up the volume for Lindoro's aria in Rossini's *L'Italiana in Algeri*.

"Will we ever break out of the 'clockwork imbecility' Gadda wrote about?"

I have to tell him the truth.

FROM THE NOTEBOOK OF PASSING DAYS

Days of June, beside the river.

A little boy came to see me. I found him at the door of my house in Po. He looked at me very hard, as if he needed to report the details of our meeting to someone else. His cheeks were very red, he seemed sweet. He had a bunch of flowers in one hand, an envelope in the other. He gave them to me and then ran away, stopping only long enough to tell me . . .

"I'm Giuliano, her nephew."

I opened the envelope. The note said, "I'll wait at the Blue Bar. Tonight. Like in the song that says the moon's a wandering soul." No name, no need for one. I knew who she was.

I started walking into the darkness when the moon was just starting to make its way, like a melancholy regret you can't really explain. I took the road that led to the Blue Bar. I remembered the little zoo on the left, just before the embankment. It was still there. The zoo's guests had barely fallen asleep in their astral silence; a few feathers floated here and there, among the cages: the ones from the birds of paradise seemed fragments of diamonds in the lunar light.

I walked until that hour of the night when the wicker chairs are stacked up in front of the cafés, and you see the pile growing, one on top of the other, like the thoughts in your head, and they drop the metal shutters down, echoing, implying that the huge idea that is life might only merit a noisy curtain coming down.

The moon had swung to its highest place when we sat down across from one another. We were alone, among all the wicker chairs, and it was almost as if we could taste the flavor of what miraculously seemed to us the most perfect full moon we had ever seen.

We touched each other's hands:

"Ciao, Ada."

She didn't say anything. She bent her head and squeezed my hands.

Years had passed, but she was more than ever the Ada Vitali of the time when Ligabue proclaimed that hers was the most beautiful sex anywhere along the river Po, celebrating it, carving it into the trunk of a poplar, and then kneeling down, worshipping it as if it had not been he who created it but nature herself who was at that moment offering him the joyous gift that the living woman had always refused him.

Ada, the first woman to make room for me in a bed, at her side . . .

In the village of scythes.

We let a long time go by, always on the point of speaking words to each other, never uttering them. We understood that it was beautiful to stay there like that, with words at the tip of our tongue, too many for any conversation to contain.

When dawn began to break, we saw along the crest of the hill the boatmen's tow-horses, all in a line against the horizon, following the lead horse in solemn obedience, the only one with a rider on his back. Almost without our noticing, we had gone further downriver to where flights of red herons suddenly rose up with the sun, leaving glaring sands behind them and turning the sky to cupolas the color of blood.

We stopped at the point where the sea waves struggle against the river current, wrinkling the surface, creating the illusion that the water is flowing backwards, going upstream instead of toward the mouth.

And our two lives were something like that, because of how we felt inside.

Then, only then, Ada Vitali asked:

"I was beautiful once. Wasn't I?"

I think of Misia.

She was one of the most fascinating women of the century. Although she passed from one love to the next, and although her marriages gave her wealth and social prestige, she succeeded in maintaining her freedom. The inspiration for artists of the dance, she was the only participant in Diaghilev's drama to remain close to him, to mourn him and weep. It was she who most lucidly understood the unhappy hero of the *Ballets Russes*, Vaslav Nijinski.

I think of my lost life. And of how much of it might not have been lost if I had had a woman like Misia beside me.

THE EROS OF REMORSE

Once more, images of that peripheral neighborhood that doesn't seem Roman. Façades that have outlived the rest of the building, courtyards and rows of arches that float over nothingness, bricked-up doorways that suggest the idea of secret rooms although behind them is the void. Everything seemed to have crumbled or sprung up by accident in the squalor of the countryside. Light fell like a cut from big purplish clouds.

Whenever I went to Alessandra's I had the feeling that she was inhabiting ruins on an island which had been superimposed, by natural magic, on the layers of the capital.

Soon I would hear music coming from her windows, signaling her house hidden by a row of trees. The music arrived and I recognized it. It was a *Concerto Grosso* by Boccherini, one of her favorites.

"Boccherini's *wavelength* expresses me," she would say, with her passion for analogy.

I thought of her studies in history and philology, her love for the myths of the Greek world. These would have guaranteed her a solid academic reputation if she hadn't lived by gambling her personal success against her love for the game itself. She used to tell me, "The great lesson of Greek civilization is that art flourishes, mysteriously, in splendor and in misery, in liberty and in slavery." For her, I was an artist. And I supported myself as such, in fact, under wildly diverse conditions.

She had believed in me, pushing me to believe in myself. With her exuberant and eccentric character, she had stimulated my anarchic and intolerant side.

A single reproof of hers upset me bitterly: for abandoning myself to the vice of getting depressed, giving up, and then tormenting myself over having given up.

But the vicious don't follow advice.

Alessandra fascinated me with her mental and sentimental vitality. She brought me the seeds of stories, involving me in surprising situations, even in love affairs with women who were friends of hers. She never knew jealousy and she always introduced me to other friends of hers, convinced that my curiosity should devour everything, thus avoiding being transformed into unhappiness which would otherwise have devoured me.

"You have to see things the way they are," she insisted, "stop making everything into a myth."

"You, of all people, tell me that? You who've made the great myths the whole reason for your life?"

She answered me clearly: "Yes, I do tell you that. And this is why: the true voyage that a man has to accomplish is through his myths, to free himself from them."

Alessandra continued to telephone me even after my decision to break off with everyone who, as she did, tried to entice me out of the lair of my depression and isolation. I didn't want to listen to her anymore. Not even when, during her last calls, she sounded different, almost as if she wanted to ask me for help. Another of her smart tricks, I thought. How silly to think Alessandra, who helps everyone else, would ever need to ask for help, and with that tone of sadness that she'd never used before. One day when I was in a foul mood I hung up on her, and after that, all contact ceased.

∾

. . . I came into her garden. Angela B. came out to meet me. She was her secretary, her companion. "My diligent scribe," Alessandra explained. "If anything of me remains, I'll owe it to her. She writes everything down, whether I'm talking about Mediterranean myths or improvising some personal plot. But she doesn't know that I poke around in her diaries, too."

I was happy to see Angela, too. She gave me her hand. She hesitated.

"Do you really want to see Alessandra?"

I didn't understand.

She beckoned me to follow her. We went up the stone steps, stood at the closed door. Angela rang the bell, repeatedly. No one answered. Finally Alessandra's hand emerged between the panels. On her fingers, the ring I had given her threw out reflections. Several times the fingers spread out and contracted, like a bird's wing.

That gesture was repeating: go away.

"It's me," said Angela, in the tone one uses to a child.

The door closed. Angela's head drooped; she sighed. "Now she'll open it, you'll see."

And in fact, the door opened. But Alessandra didn't appear. Angela took me into the living room, among the cages of birds I recognized, hanging all around us.

They were of different varieties. I looked at her desk, covered with a desolate-looking cloth: it used to be heaped with manuscripts, books, journals.

I felt a presence behind me and I turned and looked. Alessandra was sunken in an armchair. From her look, aimed beyond me, I understood that she was awaiting explanations from invisible intruders. Angela spoke to her:

"Excuse us, we won't stay long."

As if she were speaking to the void.

Alessandra was wearing a robe, which hung open. I glimpsed a nudity that was still fresh, sensual; her body had kept all its charm intact, in contrast with the lines on her face, suddenly old. The music stopped. Alessandra opened her mouth from time to time, trying to communicate something, with a bewildered expression.

I came close to her and touched her. The skin of her arm was chilly. Suddenly a window blew open and a draft tossed the birds against the bars of their cages. I felt a vertigo of reds, violets, yellows, blacks.

Alessandra asked, "Where?"

Angela gave me a look.

Alessandra asked again, "Who?"

Angela murmured, "You really didn't know?"

I was stunned. The question came out of me painfully:

"How long has she been like this?"

"For a year. Six months ago she got much worse. She had a stroke one night. She isn't getting better."

Near my head, a little bird was pointing his beak at us from his cage, still and silent amid the twitterings of the others. I remembered when Alessandra had told me, "He's a white ballerina, a wagtail. The male still hasn't sung. That means he's sick." The male was sulking behind the female. All I needed to do was strum the bars of his cage slightly, as I had seen Alessandra do, for the two birds to burst into a duet. The male suggested a few notes which were quickly reprised by the female. They alternated with such perfection that, if the daylight hadn't been so bright, one would have thought that day was breaking at that moment, perhaps only inside their little prison.

I closed my eyes. It was if I were seeing again the many moments of love between myself and Alessandra, she always so full of life, to the point of excess. That was how we kindled one another, like the white birds' duet.

Beyond the clouded thoughts, something must have reawakened in the memory of the friend I had neglected. I tried to read it in her look. Whatever it might be — devastated mental images, emptiness — it made her go back in time. Her look, now fixed on mine, was touched by a smile that goes back to the first steps of our existence, to which we return when life is about to be extinguished, and there we find intact the childish feelings that have never left us.

"I'm here," I told her. "Do you know me?"

Only that smile in her eyes.

I said my name to her again. A flash in her eyes answered me. And then, on those remote pupils, the heaviness of two tears formed, which coexisted with the smile and gave the idea of resisting, trying not to exceed the confines of the eyes, weeping with an unconscious delicacy and discretion.

Her left cheek was wet. I who had always feared madness was being urged by Alessandra herself to set myself free from this phobia, in the name of a joyous plenitude. And now here madness is, in a form that could happen to me, too: I was seeing it, concretely, in the liquid line that shone between her wrinkles; the organic residue of a mind that had been lost to itself after great exuberance.

Angela drew near with a comb and a mirror. She combed her hair lovingly. Alessandra looked in the mirror, perhaps without seeing herself. But for one moment she must have glimpsed one of our amorous encounters, because the quick and unexpected kiss she left on the mirror, in a halo of breath, was certainly for me.

Then Angela closed the shutters. We were in the garden again. It took great effort to walk heavily away, while I listened:

"All Alessandra can say is 'Where?' or 'Who?' Questions that don't mean anything. Sometimes strange melodies come out of her, as if she were answering the birds. The doctors say I should keep playing the music she used to love. Sometimes the sounds seem to make her more . . . conscious."

I started to leave. Then Angela added, "She tried to find you, when she could still communicate. Before that night, the last telephone call she made was to you."

"Are you telling me that I could have helped her in some way?"

"She was worried. She was afraid you might have just disappeared, that someone might hurt you, that you weren't working anymore. She believed in you as in no one else, and she wouldn't ever have wanted you to have any reason to suffer."

WOMEN OF DORADUS

Worshippers of the phallus. Phallophores. Phallophoria was an ancient Dionysian rite, a procession that accompanied the simulacrum of the phallus.

For some women, that rite has never died. The mythic procession continues in their heads. They judge a man by the proportions of his member, follow the bestial appendage, chitchat about it with their friends, can't rest until they capture it.

I call them scornfully the *Women of Doradus*.

Doradus is a nebula in the Magellanic Cloud, the next galaxy to ours. It contains an "abnormal" star, supermassive, three thousand times our sun's mass. It's one of the anomalies of the cosmos, surrounded by a magnetic field, and astronomers define the stars drawn into it as "desolate and disharmonious."

Antiquity has left us countless traces of phallic adoration: Egyptian obelisks, the monuments of Delos, the Female Phalloi of Sireuil, the ithyphallic figures of Altamira or Isturitz, bas-reliefs of the Magdaleine, Corsican monoliths, certain oblong stones pounded into the earth at Cuzco or in the Indies, Polynesian constructions, Macedonian coins, Etruscan tombs, in addition to — of course — the orgiastic religion of Dionysos.

Superstitions: in Spain and among Mohammedans, pregnant women used to invoke a powerful protection from evil by kissing the abnormal sexual parts of a madman. Ceremonies of cruelty: even the ancient Egyptians castrated their conquered enemies and heaped up the severed phalli to have an exact count of the victims of their military glory, estimating that a man without a penis was a dead man. Along the Po, until just a few years ago, a bull used to be castrated to prevent floods. The women would invoke Bio, the phallic god, until the beast's semen burst forth in the greatest possible quantity, to be then splashed on the river bank; thus — they assured me — placating the flood. The ceremony required that blood be splashed, too. The ground became vermilion. Women fought over the amputated rod.

The Women of Doradus have the *olisbos* in their soul. The *olisbos* is the artificial penis of huge dimensions with which, by order of the male members of the family in ancient Greece, young girls were initiated into lovemaking in Thasos. Sappho, a teacher in Thasos, fled from this horror. And Aristophanes speaks of a "Virile simulacrum made of boiled leather, formerly used by the crude and degenerate women of Milétos."

174

In contrast to female adoration of the phallus we might consider "vagina dentata," a psychoanalytic locution that defines the male's obsessional fear that his own member may be consumed by a castrating woman; this obsession is linked to the image of the frightful mother, and to a monstrous constellation of omnivorous spiders, Jonah's whales, animals like those conceived by Bosch and Grandville. The dread of castration returns in certain neurotic subjects confronted by the female sexual organ: to introduce the phallus, an object of veneration, into a mysterious body which is also perceived as hostile, provokes panic and disgust in them. In many cases, active homosexuality leads to the penetration of a male body which appears neither mysterious nor insidious since it is similar to his own. The female orifice, however, is an unthinkable mortal cavity.

The Doradus-Women who remain either secretly or openly at the phallic stage have always provoked commiseration in me. I see them proceed along a bare hillside, perhaps at Phaïstos or Knossos, unique celebrants in a phallophoria cloaked in a cloud of ash.

There was a time when my house seemed like a desert.

One day I climbed up the hundred and twenty steps of the spiral staircase that led to the restoration of the Correggios inside the cupola of the cathedral of Parma, and I found myself next to angel musicians who were exchanging kisses and embraces as they flew. They possessed the same carnal magic as the women I love best. Only among the ruins of Knossos and of Phaïstos, in the Cretan light, had I found the same physical and spiritual solidity, coupled with a perception of the myth of origin; the same imagination, filled with the "azure dolphins of the gynaeceum" brought to the invention its own feminine art.

Thus I could recognize myself in the angel musicians. I too, genetically, had had the heightened colors of restoration kneaded into me: the pale rose of morning, shades of violet, the boundless white of clouds. The acrid breath that came out of the frescoes struck me so powerfully that I felt the dizziness of those figures passing from earth to heaven. This was no mystical triumph. It was an immersion in the cupola's inverted abyss. The angels were going up to God while forgetting about him and the reason for his Creation. For God's own pure optical pleasure.

I reached out my hands, I touched their bodies. But at the very moment I made that gesture, night fell suddenly over backs, crotches, armpits, legs stretched out to clasp other legs. Under my fingertips there was darkness. And I, even with my fingernails touching that heaven, felt the sensation of falling into emptiness and shadows . . .

It happened like that with my favorite women. Night would fall. I could no longer manage to have the kind of encounters that illuminate a lifetime in a more or less brief moment. It happens.

In such emptiness, I still needed someone to reach out to me, to invade me. Even the worshippers of the phallus who came to me: girls and women who for the most part went to discothèques, hung out at clubs, looking for the maxiprick, as they laughingly told me. I remember one of them, Daniela, telling me:

"I find myself falling in love not with men as persons, but with their erect god. I'm talking about men who lie down on a bed and look really pleased at the gift they got from the god they carry around in their shorts. This excites them more than I do. Then they notice that I'm there, and they penetrate me. I've had every kind inside me. It's a shame, I know, that I almost never think of a face, or of how someone might have been able to talk to me, understand me, console me . . . But I've got a different religion."

Staring at nothing, she told me, "There's one guy named Maurizio . . ."

I didn't see her for several months.

She came back one Sunday afternoon. Her eyes were red and puffy, like those of people who suffer from long insomnia. I often think about that day . . . I touched her forehead: it was burning. She looked at me, dazed, trying to keep her eyelids open over the dullness of her gaze. She let her head fall back, telling me she'd like to sleep for a month, a year. She spoke of sleep as an impossible liberation, overcome with a desperation I had guessed:

"It used to be so easy to sleep. Now I feel as though I've never slept at all."

She undressed, she got under the covers; only her eyes showed, still red, looking at me. She started to tell me that if I wanted to make love to her she'd really try to stay awake. I reassured her:

"Sleep. Don't worry about it."

She fell instantly asleep. I enjoy being awake next to a sleeping woman. Usually even the most unhappy ones assume positions that take them back through time: to infantile serenity, to their first loves. And so their hands clasp between the thighs, almost as if they were protecting the sex like a precious treasure. Even in sleep sentiment persists.

Then someone began ringing the doorbell insistently.

The young man, about thirty, came in without hostility, saying he was Maurizio, the one Daniela had confessed to me that she loved because of his arrogant god. He came into the living room, immediately taking possession of it. No explanations were needed. One look from him had informed me that I had no right to say anything, for the simple reason that he was about to discover, here in my house, a woman who used to be one of his.

In short, I was the one who didn't belong. With a thief's instinct, he divined where the bedroom was and went straight in there, shoving me aside. I followed him, entreating:

"Let her sleep. She's sick."

I saw him yank the covers off her. Daniela was lying in the fetal position I had imagined, fists closed, oblivious to everything. I felt vindictive and tense, perfectly cold, like the invader who was ordering her to get dressed, get up. Trying to make her stand, he grabbed her by the neck and under the arms, but it was no use.

Under the weight of her obviously drugged sleep, the girl fell back down onto her knees. He slapped her. Nothing happened. Now he was striking her blindly, with growing fury.

～

The girl didn't seem to feel pain, even when he punched her vagina. Her eyelids opened for a moment, but she didn't make any connection.

At this point, the scene changed from cruel to repugnant. Peering vaguely at the man who was abusing her violently, she had an automatic reaction. The instinct to defend herself and also to obey his tyrannical imperative. She opened her mouth under the male's spread legs. Her fleshy, lipstick-smeared lips narrowed into an obscene circle which stayed unmoving and out of which her tongue flicked before it flopped onto her teeth.

The invader hesitated, staring at the gaping mouth; then he lowered his zipper and, he too obeying a conditioned reflex — not of desperation but of brutality — extracted his member and stuffed it in. Nausea sent me away with my brain vacant. I found myself in the kitchen, in front of the sink. From the window behind me, an icy light fell on the knife I had pulled out of the rack.

The drip of the faucet marked a beat: inertia or impatience, I couldn't tell. The knife was there, within reach. I took hold of it as I heard the invader go into the bathroom. It was as if I could see him urinating, naked and sulky. He came quickly back into the bedroom, slamming the door. The idea of killing a man no longer seemed absurd . . .

I came back into the bedroom too. I put the knife against the young man's neck, telling him serenely, "If you don't leave, I'll kill you."

❦

I wasn't aware of moving the blade. A thread of blood came down the shoulder of the creature I considered less than a worm I might step on. He could have fought me. He was lighter, stronger than I. I didn't even care, actually; the idea that he might try excited me, if anything. But instead I discovered that these idols of the Doradus-Women are cowards in whom even fear causes dull erections. The invader fled. I smoothed the covers over Daniela's body, and, with a fleeting and grateful smile, she went back to sleep.

❦

...and there have been others. "Women of Doradus!" I would scold them, and they would laugh, not understanding.

The wretchedness of my solitude made an ally of scorn. I would let them come to me, often toward dawn, returning from clubs, just so I could fit them into some context, despise them, see how they act, take pity on them.

They were poor wanderers. They would disseminate their undergarments here and there, rummage around, make a mess of my things. They used to talk and talk about their investigations, their verifications, defeats, their obsessions. I became a master of feigned attention. Eros for them was a battlefield or a frozen lake where they spun on skates, executing obligatory figures.

Let them keep doing it. Let them turn my house inside out like a glove. It's one way of exorcizing the void, the fixation. Anyway, with patience, I could always put everything back the way it had been. In sexual relations they didn't know that in reality they were conjoining themselves with those walls, those ceilings, all those

179

things immersed in the same desolation as the man upon whom they bent their entomologists' gaze, simply gratified by the presence of an anatomy. To provoke my sick interest, they would attribute perversions to themselves, smoking and tracing bizarre trajectories in the dark with the embers of their cigarettes. They used to tell me how they sought satisfaction by yielding to the most humiliating experiences, and about the uterine furor that led to obsessive complications and gave birth to anecdotes of ferocious sarcasm: about some men's fears or the exasperating narcissism of others.

They would leave in broad daylight. From the bed, I watched them get dressed. A kiss and goodbye. I belonged to my own loneliness again. I emptied the ashtrays. I changed the sheets and pillowcases, damp with sweat and reciprocal liquids. Many of them forgot their lighters, bracelets, earrings, sunglasses. If I lay down again, it was for the pleasure of lighting my cigarettes with those lighters, putting on sunglasses that didn't belong to me.

Perched on my nose was a way of looking at reality through eyes which just a little while ago I had seen scrutinizing a man's anatomy as if it were the only reason for life.

FAREWELL TO A. B.

It's an evening like all the others; Rome, the way it always is.

But, for us, a sunset light, more human than men or things, rises up to divide day from night, and fill the space around us. That hour of magic is suffused with a kind of mystery, suggesting things unseen.

We can hear the silence essential to true communication, the rests between spoken words and city noises, and the natural splendor there, like a breath.

We try to take deep breaths, breathing in the "something" that's existed between us until now.

I urge her, "Turn out the light. Let the darkness be complete. I don't want to see you leave. I don't even want to see your shadow under the star trembling up there in the window, curious about us, hurrying into the night which is more patient than she is . . . We've talked for so long, I've confessed myself to you, as if you were my image in the mirror, part of me . . . Please, just disappear like that, with the lights out, like all the hopes that have vanished into me."

"Even when you've had reversals of fortune, fate turns out to have been kind to you."

"But time's going by so quickly, my dear love . . ."

"Time, yes . . ."

"Once you've gone from here, send me some greeting from far away. Call out my name with the clarity we've spoken of, diminishing like one of those light voices in the silence that used to fill up my Emilian countryside when I was a boy questioning the clouds that stretched out above the paths where couples, lovers, would disappear around bends in the road where the mulberry trees were thickest. . . ."

"Hush, we're both going to be fine."

"There are moments when I'm so afraid; and I know what the mongoose feels when the cobra. . . ."

The light goes out behind A. B.'s beautiful profile.

She had been like one of those birds of passage who rests on my terrace high above Rome, in their flight towards mysterious lands. They leave me a hint of their mystery. Just as A. B. has left me some of hers.

"I thank you," I tell her, "for the delicacy with which you've helped me bring order to my memories and desires, the actions that still keep on involving me. . . ."

In the absolute darkness, a caress brushes me. The door shuts with a soft click.

How cruel, I think, the felicity of gratitude can be, when you know that a woman has deserved the full force of your remembrance forever.

A HAPPY FRAGMENT

Eros is also a detail of memory that seizes you one morning when you least expect it, and you walk on, carrying your loneliness into the mystery of a little side street. Something said by a woman you once loved returns to your ear. It seems to give a meaning to the lost days of your whole life:

" . . . you were the first with whom I felt like a woman. Making love with you, all the tormenting dissension, between the attraction and the difficulty of letting myself go, ceased. At last I could have a feeling for the sexual act, dominate it, discover that if it is dominated, it opens the way to absolute feeling.

"You asked me to undress, and I was already receiving an erotic message I could translate into my own serene complicity, opening doors to an intimacy that had usually closed in on itself with the men I'd known before. . . ."

WHORES

Everything looks so serene and tranquil in the soft sunlight that caresses the corners of the houses, with sparrows chattering in the
cupolas of trees, that the cool whistling that comes from a door beside the main entrance to the jail seems perfectly in character. I'm
waiting for someone. The first thing I see is his hands, cupped to
shield the flame of a lighter, then a head that's hidden by the very
act of lighting a cigarette, then at last the shape which, from the
way it moves, can only belong to one man: the Sultan.

Emitting a first puff of smoke, Mario, also known as the Sultan,
gaily greets the prison guards (he's serving a three year sentence,
he's approaching the end of his jail time, so he can come out during the day but he has to go back inside at night). He comes up to
my car, going around it, stopping where he can't be seen, next to the
open window. I had met him years ago, when I was a crime reporter for *Il Messaggero*.

He was the last great impresario of Roman prostitution.

He wanted to see me, talk to me. Prostitutes — he calls them "my
ladies in waiting, my favorites" — are coming back into newspaper
stories which by now have become a bottomless well: they gobble
up every pretext for scandal, however false or pathetic. There was
even a film called *Le buttane* at the Cannes Film Festival.

There are rumors about reopening the Houses of Love. The
Sultan has even read declarations by prestigious writers like
Naipaul: "I had a tremendous, unsatisfied sexual thirst. I wanted to
learn the physical art of seduction. I was a great client of whores."

Vidiadhur Naipaul, anglo-Indian, many times candidate for the
Nobel prize, until yesterday famous for his ill-tempered reserve
and the inflexibility with which he refused to indulge the curiosity
of journalists who wanted to write about his private life. Therefore

his confession, in an interview granted to the *New Yorker*, was sensational and made the front pages of newspapers everywhere.

The Sultan, who has a face like a weasel's, tosses his cigarette away, shrugs. "Too much fuss. Too much talk . . . I've got to say it, and it breaks my heart: my world is finished. Just like operetta. Now we're supposed to be happy with special effects." And to confirm his notion, he quotes from his favorite work, "Friend, 'that fleeting hour' just ended; nobody gets to drain the cup of pleasure any more!"

He leans his elbow on the window, looks me in the eye as he affirms that, anyway, the whores of the streets and brothels are a thousand times more worthy than the women I've called *the Meccano set*, who give themselves to everyone, who go from one man to another, betraying all of them, from the shelter of their lives and in secrecy, keeping up appearances within their social rôles.

". . . They're an infestation, they're spreading like an oil slick. They're our real competition, friend. Not the crazies and the transvestites, at least they're risking their lives. But what do those others risk? They don't even put their conscience on the line. For them a conscience isn't anything alive."

We nod agreement and take our leave. The Sultan starts to walk away, whistling again; he stops and turns back:

"Hey, friend, have you ever gone back to the Sultan's Palace?"

This was his last brothel, the most prestigious among many he had set up. He considered it his royal domain, the *Maison Dorée* that mirrored his astonishing fantasy life: in his own way both inspired and vile.

The Sultan's Palace. The building, now deserted and in ruins, had enjoyed great fame as a locus of delights.

I took M. there, a young woman who is intelligent and full of curiosity, attracted by true and carnal tales. She insisted on coming.

I could see she was already fascinated as we came into the weed-grown courtyard which evoked something between a harem and an army barracks. It was early evening. The last sunlight poured through the arches.

The blue flowers that ran along the portico on the left were shaped like daisies, and that didn't surprise me, because that was where Ines Bartoli used to sit, waiting in a rattan armchair. She was known as the Dark Lady of the Waterlilies, not only because of her Hispanic-Mantuan looks, but also because she had thrice tried to drown herself in the river in the grip of a nervous breakdown that exploded in the springtime. And three times she had miraculously not been drowned because branches caught her clothes and held her up, while giant waterlilies encircled her and made her understand, just in time, that life isn't really so ugly if it contains such fragrance.

We went up the Stairway of the Scribes. Here, too, the steps were crumbling. The humidity brought an odor of rotten apples bursting out of the walls. But we could still read a few inscriptions left there by some of the most devoted clients, who — as I explained to M. — fell into various categories: suits, tiritiri (big talkers), nostalgia buffs, softies, passion papas, and planning commissioners (sexual deviants).

I was struck by reading phrases from famous men: "Love's most beautiful moment comes as we go up the stairs." A bit further on: "Enter here, friend of my heart." Who could have known Clemenceau or Stendhal?

We went on toward the rooms. They were the kingdom of dust which, yes, had covered everything, but had exercised a kind of surprising delicacy in the way it had drifted, a respect for the forms it covered. A dust, one might say, that displayed the taste of the period that created it. In the thread of light that came through the closed shutters, its hues varied, with little pools of color here and there, like the leaves and arcane flowers of a vegetation that had never been profaned. M.'s youthful profile was heartbreaking against that ray of light.

Before stepping inside and opening the windows, I tell her, "We can play a game. . . ."

"What game is that?"

"Ah, you could become each one of the women I tell you about. Their humiliations and fantasies. I could be, for every one of them, a different client?"

I suggest this to her as a joke that contains a hint of farewell that M. doesn't pick up: it's impossible, at her age. Nonetheless, the game both troubles and amuses her.

The first room is where Maddalena lived, whom everyone called "*E lucean le stelle*," the starry night. Her claim to fame was a pair of wetnurse's breasts, two volcanoes of milk, and she, as a girl, had gone through the countryside, from farm to farm, suckling new-born babies.

Later she passed to adults, convinced that the hearts of men never outgrow their newborn state, and she was capable of nurturing an entire company of *bersaglieri*, soldiers who doffed their feathered caps and crouched on her lap, like the little child in Giorgione's *Tempest*, and as they sucked they kept on saying, I don't want to go to war. . . .

Coming in and seeing the white flash of those breasts, swollen with an infinity of milky ways, the habitués would say, "*E lucean le stelle*."

⤌

Young M. played at being Maddalena for me.

The second room was known as *A t'è capì?* ("Get it?") in honor of Virginia Mori, from Emilia, who as the act ended, asked everyone "Get it? Do you understand?" What the hell is there to understand, they always said, pulling their pants up. But she would repeat the question with such a tigress' glare that they might have a sudden doubt, standing there holding their pants, staring at *A t'è capì?*, her queenly body already squatting over the bidet, while they asked themselves: was there really something I was supposed to understand, wasn't I just porking around?

The Sultan had to intervene: "You've got to quit that, Virginia, because they come here for exactly the opposite, they come here to not understand, okay?"

"Okay, right, I understand," said *A t'è capì?*.

"Someday we'll understand something for you, Virginia, we'll understand and make you happy."

With her little girl's look, M. suggests, "I understand what you're trying to tell me."

I stroke her head with a bitter smile which she really couldn't understand, "Maybe . . ."

Then came the rooms called "The Roman Girls'" because in each of them lived a Roman woman who had a life of her own, if it could be called that, meaning something more than making love for pay and something beyond normality.

We went into Laura's room, she who was nicknamed "Where it hurts," both because of the pain she had endured in life and because of her distinctive specialty. The tongue between her lips had been trained by hunger. Her mother, her mother's mother, and all the mothers of their mothers, had reacted to food with the same initial wonder and then later the same avidity that Laura brought to sex with men or women. Because this Roman woman had known every stark bitterness of life, her tongue knew how to soothe the exact spot where the symbolic tooth of sensibility ached in her lovers, and she sent them all away consoled, until she retired, resigned, into her own ache, the pain that no one could ease.

. . . And M. became Laura.

This room was Lydia's, called "The lighthouse in the empty sea." She was a Roman of scrawny body, apparently without the slightest seductive charm. Her looks were totally unmemorable. If you didn't know, and if you saw her sitting around in her lilac bathrobe, you'd ask yourself what in the world she was doing in the Sultan's Palace.

But there at the base of her bony pelvis, her sex, the lighthouse itself, exploded in its magnificence, like the unhoped-for source of light that revives the heart of the shipwrecked sailor in the desolation of the sea. It heightened all the rest of her with a kind of magic, proving that the body has its own language to be learned and practiced.

... M., too, has a glorious sex.

And here is Pupa's room, "The Little Sister." Pale blonde hair, an ecstatic expression on her face, she waited, sitting on a stool between the light and the shadows. When you saw her, she seemed to be the perfect dream image of childhood, an ambiguous smile on her lips, the look of someone having a vision: her eyes were the ones we see in photographs of children who died soon after the picture was taken. And as a child Pupa had died the death of the heart, because she had been raped in a particularly terrible way. Thus she never hesitated to satisfy the basest dregs of men's desires, while keeping for herself her dream of freshness.

It sometimes happened that the servants and even the Sultan himself had to rush to her, frightened by the shrieks that twisted that body of hers, formed for girlish games. Dawn would find her bed ripped apart, sheets and pillows on the floor, broken toys, overturned chairs, traces of blood on sharp instruments.

M. grasped all this: this is the childhood we carry inside us, half Little Sister, half demon when awakened by the poisonous snake of violence.

And at last Clizia, "The Nightbird." Certain clients were madly excited by the bird and animal cries she uttered, which suggested to them that she must have had relations with animals, too. And she did, indeed, but not in the way they thought. She fervently believed that men were beasts, but without the grace of real animals, those elect among God's creatures, and since she also believed in God, she dedicated her best self, that scrap of soul remaining to her, to helping animals.

Her most hopeless love had been for a red crossbill, the prince of nightbirds. But one day he flew away forever. Hopping across a rooftop at sunset, he happened to come beak to beak with a female of his own species, causing his heart to beat faster, as did the female's, it being a caprice of God's for two red crossbills of different gender to meet on the rooftiles of a city so far from their native forest, warmed, however, by a sun that contained the languors of the remote land of their birth.

They fell madly in love and flew away to their long-lost land.

. . . we were looking out the window. A huge moon shone over the Roman rooftops.

M. told me, "May our dreams save us and guide us."

SOME REQUIRED STOPOVERS BEFORE THE END . . .

I've come back to the pensione in Via Valadier.

I spent two of the hardest years of my life there, when I first came to Rome to work at *Il Messaggero*.

I ask for a room. The manager, Emma Allegri, from Sermide in the Padana region, is still the same. The years haven't changed her. She recognizes me at once and welcomes me, tells me she sees me on television and reads my books (obviously untrue: her reading is limited to police reports and citations for the ambiguous clientele she has in her rooms). She's happy that I've come back to see her, to "sojourn" at her place, according to an expression she likes to use, even it's just for one night.

"Sojourn." Nothing has changed.

The *pensione* was fabricated by putting up walls in rooms that were too big, something you also find in old apartment buildings in Prati. She has arranged little rooms where illicit and clandestine couples used to and still do come, and also newlyweds on honeymoon, without enough money to pay for a better place.

Often, too, the *pensione* served as a house of assignation for "*belles de jour*": "straight" wives of professional men, girl students, some of them very young; legal secretaries. What some apparently irreproachable women are capable of doing in secrecy cannot be imagined.

Still, Emma Allegri has had, and continues to have, her troubles with the law.

I was the only resident who had nothing but my own imagination as a clandestine or illicit companion. I knew everything about every couple who came there. Of that sampling of humanity, I registered intimate habits and preferences with an ease that at first surprised me. I would come back late at night from the paper, carrying on me the smell of the crimes I had investigated in the most sordid places: murders, suicides, bloody fights. That odor of blood and extreme squalor. And it seemed to me that I could purify myself, reawaken my lust for existence, by coming out of my room into the shadowy hallway.

I passed by rooms where excessive, difficult, maniacal loves were being enacted; the corridor wound among women who had fled their homes or been thrown out, who were being tracked down or who were looking for a way to escape, and men who possessed them with brutal vulgarity, deceived them, and mostly maltreated them.

Why did I keep staying at the "Valadier"? I seized as a pretext the fact that Emma charged me a ridiculously low rent and that I liked her eccentricities (Sermide, her home town, is known for the grandfather clocks made there; she had one enthroned in the dining room, its hands stopped, pointing up at the ceiling, perhaps to illustrate that clandestine love knows no time). In reality, I found it stimulating that all those comings and goings involved me while leaving me outside of them.

I repeat: it's all as it was before. Tonight, too.

When one of the lovers goes down the hall to the bathroom, the door is not quite closed. I glimpse the bodies of waiting women, or men who are smoking, staring at the air.

I know the rituals being performed and I still wince at female cries, slaps on the buttocks, stifled oaths.

I watch, I listen, as when I imagined the labyrinth of Eros for the first time, not knowing it didn't exist, and that whoever wanders therein is lost in anguish. In some situations imagination is of no use. How could I exchange any fantasy for the reality of those rooms marked with a number five or seven or nine? In the latter, a man about fifty, bald, suspicious even when he's eating or watching television, was raging inside a woman who kept weeping. He grabbed her by the hair, knocking her against the wall. He forced her to perform the actions and poses of some pornographic photos he consulted. I heard him saying "Fogna! Sewer, cesspool!" over and over behind the door.

I turn toward the end of the corridor. There is still just one bathroom. A lightbulb sheds icy white light over the stained tiles. I turn off the light, leaving the door ajar, and I sit on the edge of the tub. Light comes through the window which gives onto an interior courtyard. My heart is beating with anticipation and with fear. From my room I heard women coming in here to shower or to use the bidet. Perhaps I'm waiting for them, or perhaps not. I'm waiting, that's all.

The men always come in with their member concealed. Whoever isn't wearing pajama pants or undershorts has a towel around his waist. They turn on the light and, seeing me, excuse themselves and leave. For their lovers, it's different. Only a few of them bother to cover themselves. They count on the rapidity with which they can reach the bath, not to mention the carnal complicity of the other guests, caught in the same situation. Some of them rush in naked. Seeing me, their heads snap back, but after the first disconcerted moment, an imperceptible conniving is present.

Unlike the men, they don't immediately leave. In their eyes I read the expert cunning that habituates certain women to subterfuge and feigned misunderstanding, in the conviction that everywhere there are men of bad faith, and that innocence is a dead end. I look at sweaty breasts; orifices which I know have just been penetrated; bare feet or slippers or high heels. Some of them are so pale, others flushed, on others yet I can see bruises and scratches. They range from boldness and rough vitality to frustration, a contrast frequently seen in clandestine loves. And you understand it from their eyes, which sparkle with perversity or are clouded with something close to tears; or from their lips, drained white or smeared with lipstick; or from the way they hold their shoulders . . .

I came back to the Pensione Valadier because it's here that my curiosity was subjected to its most violent highs and lows, and its possibilities of supremacy put to the hardest test.

Life is worthwhile because of what the reverse of the medallion shows us.

I couldn't not go there, before ending: to see my mother again, in my countryside. I've already told you: I've had the good fortune of having a witty mother. We sit down across from one another and she says: "Oíla! Look who's here!" I can come back after two days or ten years, it makes no difference. It's wonderful. She exclaims "Look who's here!", sets the table, and takes up where we left off:

"What were we talking about last time?"

I remember and so does she. And so we begin to talk again about whatever we were talking about the last time, but the world goes by so quickly, and maybe we speak about someone who was alive then but is dead now, but that doesn't matter so much to us, what matters is that the thread of our discourse hasn't died.

The last time, we were talking about "naughty" women, one of her expressions, referring to women who performed in the circuses which, here as everywhere else, are disappearing, while more clowns and inventors of tricks clutter the roads of civilization; and it's a shame because the circuses from this part of the world were fabulous, were a thousand and one nights, so much so that the circus that came to Macondo, in *One Hundred Years of Solitude*, was inspired by one that really came from Po to South America, and if you don't believe this, ask the author.

My mother begins to tell me again about Miss Pizzi, star of the Alibrandi Equestrian Circus, who would remove all her clothes while standing on the back of a white horse, never falling off, flinging garments here and there, holding them out like wings, looking like an angel, and this is still true today at the madhouse of Colorno where she is the delight of the other inmates whose day begins with Miss Pizzi, in equestrienne garb, flicking her whip; and then her riding clothes fly away, and everyone applauds, happy that they've had a show that day, too . . .

There comes a moment when my mother confides in me:

"You know they haven't forgotten me?"

I know who she means, but she always explains to me:

"The lovers I could have had. One of them still brings me

bunches of flowers and lets me know that living and waiting has been his way of holding onto youth, and so he'll keep on waiting till the very end."

She also tells me that she still keeps up her "Book of Colors," her diary without written words, in which each day that goes by has its colored mark, to remind her if it was a happy one or not.

"Ciao," I tell her, "goodbye, my mother."

FIRST LOVES

Who knows why, as we sum up a life, we remember certain early loves that memory had completely erased.

Along the river where I was born, the winters were very long. And I was happy when the winter of my fourteenth year was longer than any other, because I could venture out in the fog and frost and watch Zelia through the windows of her house. The glass was full of hanging icicles, and between the icicles just little openings that let me see inside. The ice merged into my fantasy, but it also had the power to awaken it.

Zelia was moving around inside the kitchen, passing in front of the light. I was seeing the different parts of her beautiful face, details: her hands, her mouth, her eyes, her hair that gave off a golden light. I fell in love with those details, while the rest of her body was invisible: it sank into my imagination, grew inside of me, without boundaries, like the vastness of the winter.

I remember the sound of snow falling from the branches behind me. It made me jump, as if Zelia's father, a former policeman, had found me crouching there by the window.

It wasn't just the girl's face and body that fed my imagination. The glow of a lightbulb, of the fireplace, the gleam of the glasses on the table, were all reason for me to be moved by something I couldn't even name. Then the winter ended, the sun came pouring through the branches, melting the snow. The transparent places on the windows grew slowly larger before my eyes, day after day, even though I kept praying that spring wouldn't come so quickly.

But the sun was impatient, and the kitchen, growing ever more visible, looked quite different, like certain squalid shops where you can't really tell what they might be selling there in the dust and dimness, and the flashes of light inside stopped having their wondrous halos, reminding me rather of the light on sacred wall paintings scraped away by time, leaving the Madonnas and the Christs so sad and out of place.

I found myself following Zelia, keeping out of sight, along the path beside the river. I saw her appear against the intense brightness that came up from the water, scarved with swallows and seabirds, harbingers of fine weather. We started across the bridge called Passo, where you had to be careful on the iron slats suspended over a dizzying sheer drop.

I saw that Zelia was crippled.

With every dragging step her heels rang against the iron strips with a disharmony that, as we went on across, echoed the irregular leaping of my heart, thoughts piling up like piercings through my head, out of which my dream was fleeing. Moving uncertainly, Zelia wasn't letting herself look down.

Halfway across, she swayed dizzily, and I had to run and hold her up. It was in that moment, clutching her arm, with her face mirrored in mine for the first time, that I discovered that there exists an Eros of pity.

There was once a young man named Uebi, because, they said, he
was born in Ethiopia to Italian parents. He passed his days seated
in front of the hut where he lived alone, near the sea, listening to
the sound of the waves, breathing in the smell of the sea, imagining what it might look like. He had been blind from birth, and was
of astonishing beauty . . .

Many girls climbed up the cliff by the sea where his shack was,
urged on by their desire to give themselves to Uebi. But when they
found themselves confronted by that majestic blind face which
stared at an imaginary reality wherein earthly presences dissolved
into nothingness, they felt that their own bodies, so palpable and
still, in the sexy dresses they'd put on as if Uebi could admire them,
that all this too could be dissolved into nothingness as well. And
then they ran away.

They made stupid dares and bets: which of them would be brave
enough to cross over the invisible boundary of the courtyard and
give herself to Uebi, who after all, when you really looked at him,
seemed only to be offering an infinite tenderness. But not even
Carmen di Goro, so beautiful and wild, would do it. They saw her
come sliding down the cliffside, sobbing, her hands torn and
bloody from the thorny brush.

Practical jokes were staged. To avenge themselves, not so much
upon Uebi as on their own conflicted sense of attraction and fear,
the girls would bring their lovers up there, stopping a few meters
short of the boundary of Uebi's realm. They knew he couldn't see,
but that his hearing was extraordinary; and so they insisted, "This
is where we're going to make love, right here!" Their lovers went
along with it because that was the only way they could have them,

feeling stronger than ever in the presence of a man who couldn't see, couldn't even take an unhesitating step.

The girls would pant and cry out. They stared at the boundary of nothingness and, entwined in that corner of the courtyard, they celebrated their carnival of lovemaking . . .

I have great regard for the girl who told me all this, and I ask, "And you?"

"I saw Uebi and I simply walked across the courtyard to him."

"And what happened?"

"Uebi began to stroke my forehead, just the way you did a little while ago. I let him take off my clothes and touch me, knowing that his imagination was possessing me, just as I was possessing it, giving it shape and desire. And while Uebi's hands were moving all over my body, and when I let him penetrate me, that imagination reached the height of its powers. For the first time, I knew I was a great woman, a dispenser of greatness."

We stayed silent for a while.

"Why," I ask, "did you tell me about Uebi?"

I read the answer in her eyes where a sudden emotion passes. Perhaps I should consider my love life as emblematic of how Uebi lived, and of how others treated him, the other women, especially?

And now it's she who asks me:

"What will you do?"

Thinking about my future, I'd like to answer her by saying, "My heart is breaking." And instead I tell her:

"There are times when you have to be careful with goodbye. Hearing it, saying it."

Especially when you notice that the world is there, forgetful and distracted in its surprising innocence, through who knows what unexpected state of grace, after such wanderings; and it's at that point that you try to do simple things as they ought to be done, putting out the tip of your tongue like old Maronti at Po, who used to paint vases, keeping his hand firmly around the brush so that each tiny blue dot would be perfect.

In a moment like this, where nothing is wrong, where everything turns in harmony, and no curtain is jerked awry, and even the cries of the river birds are answered by echoes rhyming from the gravelly banks, it's really risky to come to the back of the world just because you like saying goodbye.

The world, like old Maronti, might have to jump if it's taken by surprise, and then the brush's fine point makes a smear instead. And so I decide to renounce saying goodbye, also because in these matters you never know, and it might happen that goodbye isn't what needs to be said at all. I go back to my car in the dark, and I put it in neutral, making the most of coasting downhill. I let the car start off in silence, or at most with a little rattle of gravel, into the night.

The world notices nothing. With one exception.

Turning back, I catch the girl's movement, or rather her shadow in the brightness of the room upstairs. And from that small movement I understand that she alone has heard me leave, and that she jumped up quickly to see me one last time from the window.

A NOTE ON THE AUTHOR

ALBERTO BEVILACQUA is well-known in Italy for his many novels and for his films. He was born in Parma in 1934, and published his first book, a collection of short stories, when he was twenty. He has won three of Italy's most prestigious literary awards, and now lives in Rome.

A NOTE ON THE BOOK

This book was composed by Steerforth Press using a digital version of Jenson, a typeface created by Robert Slimbach for Adobe, and based on the Roman letters of Nicholas Jenson (1420-1480), and the Italic designs of Ludovico degli Arrighi (1480-1527). The book was printed on acid-free papers and bound by Quebecor Printing ~ Book Press Inc. of North Brattleboro, Vermont.